Matchmaking
Cats
of the
Goddesses

LIBRARY ZERO

Valen-Cats

Valen-Cats

A PAWSITIVELY PURRFECT MATCH MADE IN HELL

PEPPER MCGRAW

Contents

One

"THIS HAS BEEN a disaster," Tivali lamented, her tail twitching in annoyance.

"A complete nightmare," Bygul growled in agreement. He couldn't believe how poorly things were going with this latest witch.

She was supposed to be the easy one! After all, she'd already found her mate.

"Oh, it's not that bad," Soraya said. "The cats weren't too traumatized and we found each of them homes in the end, didn't we?"

"Not traumatized?" Muezza exclaimed. "That one kitten went completely psycho!"

"I said not *too* traumatized, and that only happened because the vampire tried to pet him,"

Soraya said. "Once we stopped letting the humans see the cats, things got a lot better."

"A lot better?" Tivali exclaimed. "We *still* haven't found a familiar for the garden witch. It's bad enough they keep destroying all her plants."

"It really is a bit of bad luck about her mate," Muezza said.

"We should have anticipated the vampire would be a problem," Bygul said in disgust. "I can't believe it never occurred to me."

"Well, why would it?" Soraya asked. "Hocus Purrcus lets the vampire pet him all the time."

"So does Cookie," Muezza said.

"And the hell-cat wouldn't be bothered if an entire coven of blood-suckers moved in," Tivali said.

"Exactly!" Soraya exclaimed. "Honestly, I think they're more bothered by the wolves."

Bygul licked a paw and rubbed his ear, thinking hard about their next steps. He didn't want to give up, but—

"I think we should take a break," Soraya said. "Not from matchmaking, of course, but from this particular match. We'll find Jo's purrfect familiar soon enough, but in the meantime, I have another rather urgent situation that needs our attention."

"What situation?" Bygul glared at the cat he

considered to be more of a liability than an asset in their matchmaking endeavors.

Every time they turned around, Soraya had the most impossible cat she wanted them to match. Either that or she was convinced the most ridiculous humans belonged together. Sure, she sometimes got it right, but just as often, she got it entirely wrong.

Unpredictable.

That's what she was.

"So." Soraya drawled out the word, her whiskers twitching in excitement.

That was *not* a good sign.

Whisker-twitching from Bygul or Tivali usually meant they had a brilliant idea.

Whisker-twitching from Muezza meant he either thought you were an idiot or he was getting ready for some in-depth cleaning.

Whisker-twitching from Soraya, on the other hand, was often a sign of impending disaster.

"I really want to match Jane and I have the purr-fect mate in mind for her."

"Jane," Bygul said. "Who's Jane?"

"The librarian," Muezza and Tivali chorused.

"Again? We already talked about this, Soraya," Bygul said. "She's not a witch. We need to finish the witches first. You keep sidetracking us and we'll never get this coven entirely matched."

"I know, but she's witch-adjacent."

Muezza snorted, Tivali's tail started to whip back and forth in agitation and Bygul just stared at Soraya.

When she said nothing else, he finally exploded, "*How* is a non-paranormal human considered witch-adjacent?"

"I thought you'd never ask," she exclaimed excitedly. "It turns out when Merry left Hell to come to Zero, Kansas, she built a tiny doorway between the two realms and one side of that door opens into the library where Jane works."

"Why would Merry—you know what? Never mind. I don't want to know." The daughters of Satan were just one of the many reasons Bygul wanted to finish matchmaking this coven and leave Zero, Kansas far behind.

"While that's very interesting, Soraya, what does it have to do with matching our coven of witches?" Bygul was impressed at how patient Tivali sounded when the tip of her tail was whacking the floor in a rapid, repeated pattern that betrayed her annoyance with every beat.

"Well, Merry and Tempest are witches, and Satan's

their father, and a couple of Satan's hell-kittens found their way through the doorway—"

"What?" Bygul, Tivali and Muezza shouted at the same time, but Soraya just kept talking.

"—and Jane found them, which is great because it turns out she's a cat lover, so she's decided to keep them."

"But they're hell-cats!" Bygul exclaimed.

"I don't think she knows that," Soraya said. "They're still young and they haven't shifted to their larger sizes yet."

Bygul groaned. "All right. Fine. We'd better go corral those kittens before Lucifer discovers two of his precious babies have gone missing."

"Oh, it's too late for that," Soraya said. "But it's purrfect, don't you think? Because I'm absolutely positive they're a purrfect match."

"What? Who?" Tivali exclaimed.

"Satan and Jane, of course!"

"Are you insane?" Bygul exploded.

"Sounds more like a match made in Hell," Muezza observed.

"Which makes it pawsitively purrfect for him, don't you think?"

Bygul, Muezza and Tivali just stared at Soraya in amazement. Because how could a cat—*any* cat, let alone a matchmaking cat of the goddesses—be so completely blind to the obvious?

THIS WAS ABSOLUTELY UNACCEPTABLE.

Someone had come into Hell and stolen two of his kittens.

Stolen!

From *him!*

The sheer audacity to steal from Satan, the Prince of Darkness, Lord of the Nine Realms of Hell and The Beast left Lucifer literally speechless.

He couldn't *imagine* who would have the sheer nerve to perpetrate such a crime.

Well, Tempest would.

And Merry *definitely* would.

But then, they were his daughters, so of *course*, they'd have the nerve.

They already had their own cats, though, so he couldn't imagine them coming here to steal a couple more.

Except the kittens were gone. And not just gone from Satan's home, but gone from all of Hell.

Nine realms and they weren't in a single one of them!

It was completely unfathomable that someone had ventured into Hell, grabbed two of his babies and then made it all the way out without a single hell-cat sounding the alarm.

Unless—

Maybe the kittens weren't taken at all.

Maybe they went on an adventure.

Luc couldn't imagine how two baby cats could find their way out of Hell without help, but there *were* a few Hell-Cats living in the earth realm they could have gone to visit.

Hell-Cats who lived with his daughters.

Which brought him right back to the idea that either Tempest or Merry had stolen his kittens.

He wouldn't put it past them.

At all.

Especially since he'd been visiting an awful lot lately, mostly because he enjoyed tormenting their new mates.

And now that he thought about it, he realized the two missing kittens gave him the perfect excuse to visit again.

Not that he'd needed one yet.

Ever since Tempest and Merry moved to the earth

realm and got mated there, it was a bit lonely in Hell for Luc, but at least they were happy, which was really all he'd ever wanted for them.

Even though happiness had come in the form of one of the Exiled and a damn wolf.

Not that he was complaining.

After all, he quite enjoyed showing up at his daughters' houses and freaking out their mates.

He had to admit, strange as it seemed, the pack lands in Jamesville that Merry called home were even more entertaining than the Coven House in Zero where Tempest lived.

This was entirely due to the wolves.

Wolf shifters on earth were just so damn goofy and way easier to rile up than even the weakest of the Exiled.

Torturing the wolves had honestly become the highlight of Luc's year.

This was why, even though he was pretty sure that of his two daughters, the likelier one to have planned a kitten heist was Merry (not because of the kittens or anything, but because she enjoyed watching people's heads explode, *especially* when the head happened to belong to her father), Luc decided to visit Tempest and her chameleon mate, Matthew, first.

It was always a bit insane inside the coven house,

with so many witches and cat familiars, but since Luc considered himself to be the ultimate cat daddy, he found it fairly easy to ignore the witches in favor of the cats.

This time when he visited, hoping to find Fury and Chaos playing with the other cats of the coven house, he found chaos of another kind.

Kyrie chaos.

This was not unusual.

Three, sometimes four earth realm cats were more than enough to cause chaos at any given time, but add a hell-cat into the midst, especially one as purely brilliant as Kyrie was, and well, anything could happen.

And often did.

When Luc arrived, he was just in time to witness one of the earth cats, Cookie, launching himself from the back of the sofa toward a tall bookshelf.

He barely made the distance, hooking his front paws over the top, while his hind claws scrabbled at the shelf below, knocking books and trinkets to the floor, before managing to lunge upward and land on top of the entire thing.

Clearly on a mission, Cookie proceeded to knock everything else off the top shelf, clearing a space for him to sit.

No. To crouch down in a classic hunting pose.

Luc looked up toward what the cat was hunting, then rolled his eyes.

Of course.

Every time he'd visited over the past month, Cookie had been on the same mission: to acquire one of the gems in the staff that belonged to the High Witch, Natalie.

Her own kitten, Moonbeam, had joined the hunt, so that whenever Natalie carried the staff around the coven house, Moonbeam would chase the lower gem, while Cookie would keep his eyes on the high one, always plotting different paths to reach it.

Why Cookie wanted the high one was anyone's guess.

Maybe it was the challenge of it all.

Either way, he clearly wasn't giving up anytime soon, which meant that Natalie appeared to have resorted to hiding her staff in plain sight.

Lying across the top of three bookshelves, the staff was clearly taunting Cookie.

Or maybe it was Kyrie doing the taunting, since she was sitting on the back of an armchair, watching Cookie's antics with a look on her face that clearly declared Cookie both an embarrassment *and* a source of great entertainment.

"You're not even going to try and stop him?" Luc demanded.

Kyrie gave *him* an entirely different look, one that implied he was demented.

Cookie's bottom quivered, his eyes on the gem of Natalie's staff high above his head.

"You do realize he'll never make that leap, right? He barely made the last one."

Kyrie just licked her paw and kept her eyes on the quivering cat bottom.

That was when Morana swept into the room.

She took one look at Luc, whirled and shouted back up the stairs, "Satan's in the house!"

"Again?" came a shout from upstairs.

Luc chuckled, recognizing Tempest's voice, as he walked across the room toward Cookie.

A few moments later, Tempest came barreling down the stairs, Natalie right behind her.

By this time, Luc was sitting on the couch with Cookie in his arms, having rescued him from his mission of doom, and the entire room now echoed with the sound of the cat's purring.

Kyrie, on the other hand, had been purely disgusted at the rescue and had stalked off in a fit of fury.

No worries, though.

She'd be back soon enough. None of the cats could resist Luc, not when he was in a cat-petting mood, which to be honest, was pretty much always.

"What are you doing here, Dad?" Tempest asked.

"Well, hello, my darling daughter. And how are you on this lovely afternoon?"

Tempest rolled her eyes, but then she sat down beside him and with a grin, leaned over to kiss his cheek. "It's good to see you. Again." She scratched Cookie on top of his head, causing the purrs to rumble even louder, if that were possible. "So, what's brought you here this time?"

"Fury and Chaos."

"As in you're here to cause them or—"

"Looking for them."

"I mean, it is a little chaotic here."

"A little?"

"But there's not a lot of fury to be found, unless you count Blade, but that's more fear than fury."

"Blade?"

"A vampire. He's terrified of Morana."

"It's ridiculous," Morana called from the kitchen, where she'd retreated after announcing his presence in the house. "He's a vampire, for goddess' sake! What kind of vampire's afraid of the dead?"

Tempest rolled her eyes. "Let's not get her started."

"Maybe if you hadn't decided to raise a few snakes the last time he saw you," Natalie shouted back.

"Ugh. Too late," Tempest groaned.

"I needed a bit of snake skin for a potion." Morana stamped back into the living room to glare at Natalie. "I had no idea there were so many snakes in the area, or vampires, for that matter." With that, she turned and stormed off, heading toward the back of the house.

"But you knew Blade was there," Natalie accused as she followed her, "and you did it anyway, just to mess with him."

Their voices faded as they got further away.

Luc chuckled. "Your coven is so entertaining, the necromancer in particular. I wonder what she'll raise next in her pursuit of the vampire."

Tempest let out a choking sound and he glanced at her, surprised to see a horrified look on her face.

"You think she's *flirting* with him?"

"Well, either that or she's torturing him, but considering there's not a whole lot of difference between the two—if you're doing it right anyway—I'd say it's a little bit of both."

Kyrie leapt up onto the couch at that moment.

"Ah, so you've come back, have you, love?" Luc held out his hand and Kyrie sniffed it for a moment before nudging it and graciously allowing him to pet her.

For a long moment, the only sound in the room was that of the two cats purring loudly.

"So why are you here, really?" Tempest finally asked.

Luc grinned. "I told you. Fury and Chaos. The kittens. They're missing."

"You've *lost* two hell-kittens?"

"I haven't lost them exactly. I'm sure they're around somewhere." He eyed his daughter suspiciously. She'd always been really good at projecting the innocent act. "I thought maybe they'd be here, visiting Kyrie."

"They're not even her kittens," Tempest exclaimed. "Why would they come here?"

"Because Kyrie mothers all the hell-kittens and they know it. Don't you, love?" He lifted her head, scratched beneath her chin and stared into her eyes.

After a long moment listening to the musings of one of the finest hell-cats he'd ever known, Luc heaved a great sigh. "All right, then. I guess I'll go check with Merry, but if they're not with her, I have no idea where they could have gone."

"Well, good luck, Dad. Let me know if you need

the Coven's help. We could always cast a locator spell or something."

"Eh, the more I think about it, the more convinced I become that your sister's somehow responsible. They're probably with the pack right now."

Tempest snickered. "That'll be interesting."

She wasn't wrong.

With a grin in anticipation, Luc pulled the flames of Hell around him and zipped from the Zero Coven House to the Jamesville pack lands, and more specifically into his daughter's living room there.

Merry and her wolfy mate weren't around, but her hell-cat familiars, Spike and Drusilla, were, so Luc spent the next hour playing with them and grilling them about the whereabouts of Chaos and Fury.

Unfortunately, they hadn't seen either of his kittens.

When Merry and her mate finally showed up—the latter looking extremely put out to find his father-in-law waiting in their living room—they knew nothing either.

Although Merry did have a look on her face that told Luc she might know more than she was admitting. When pressed, she finally said, "Maybe look for a tiny, enchanted doorway. It's possible one might exist that only a hell-kitten would find. Or a pixie."

Luc groaned. "Seriously? A pixie-sized doorway? Do you know what havoc they could wreak across the realms if they somehow made it out of Hell?"

"Oh, don't be such a drama queen," Merry said. "It's highly unlikely they'll find it, and even if they do, what's the worst that could happen? The pixies are a lot of fun, and let's face it. There are some realms that could really use livening up. As long as the pixies escaped in groups of seven or less, everything will be just fine."

"And if more than seven escaped?" Luc demanded.

Merry grinned. "Well, whatever happens, it certainly won't be boring!"

"You're a menace, Merry," Luc growled. "A total menace."

"Love you too, Dad."

Luc chuckled, then slung an arm around her shoulders and pulled her close. He dropped a kiss on top of her head, all while staring menacingly at her mate, who just glared back stoically.

Damn wolf was getting cheeky.

Stepping away from Merry, Luc sent her a wink, then said sternly, "I expect you both at our family dinner next week." He wrapped the flames of Hell around him and flashed home, the sight of the wolf turning sheet white, then toppling to the ground, filling him with joy as he went.

Jane didn't really know what to say in response to that, so she just offered, "Maybe the social sciences section?"

In her opinion, it was a pretty good suggestion, considering most people today were a bit zombie-like in their obsession with their devices, but the woman had just shaken her head and left. She hadn't returned.

That wasn't even the strangest request.

There was the man who'd stopped by to ask if she had an atlas detailing realm crossings. When she'd asked what he meant by realm, he'd just waved a hand and wandered the stacks on his own, peering at the spines of covers one by one.

He'd spent hours doing this before leaving empty-handed.

She *still* didn't know what a realm crossing was or why she'd been expected to have an atlas of them in her library.

Then there was the woman who popped in to ask if she had a book listing every variety of chocolate in the world.

"You mean like a chocolate cookbook?" Jane had asked faintly, a little freaked out because she'd swear the library had been empty before the woman started talking.

The bell above the door hadn't sounded and the woman hadn't come from that direction anyway. She'd appeared from the back of the stacks as if she'd been wandering there and had just come out to ask a question before returning to them.

"No, no," the woman exclaimed. "I don't want to learn how to cook. I just want to know all the different chocolate possibilities so I don't miss any while I'm here."

"I'm not sure you're going to find that answer here in the library," Jane told her. "Perhaps you should visit Zero Market."

"I already tried every variety they've got. I should probably explore beyond the boundaries of Zero." She fell silent for a moment, then announced, "I think it's time for another earth realm tradition. Road trip!"

There was that word again.

Realm.

Before Jane could press for more information, the woman whirled and headed for the door, calling over her shoulder, "Thanks for your help. If anyone asks, I've gone to visit the fairies." She flung open the door, stopped, looked back at Jane and said, "You know what the best part about a road trip is?"

Jane shook her head, speechless.

"Snacks, of course. It's a chocolate quest!" The last

word trailed behind her as she disappeared cut the door.

The silence in the library after the door closed was as loud a silence as Jane had ever heard.

It wasn't long after the woman left—a couple hours at most—that two tiny kittens came racing through the stacks, chasing each other and tumbling across the floor, acting as if they'd always lived in the library.

The weird thing was that Jane hadn't seen either one of them before the moment they hurtled out of the stacks, somehow appearing as if from thin air, just the way the woman had, right in the middle of the library.

Realm crossing, Jane remembered, and for a brief moment, speculated that perhaps one of these crossings stood in the middle of her library. This, of course, begged the question: if it did exist, *where* would it lead?

She stared at the stacks for a long moment, then shook her head—*nah*—and went back to her book.

Of course, that didn't last long, for the kittens did what any cat faced with a human whose nose was in a book would do.

One kitten leapt onto the counter and slapped a paw right down over the top of Jane's book, sending it crashing to the counter.

The second kitten leapt up and sprawled across the book, completely obscuring all the words on the page.

Jane wanted to protest—she'd been at a critical moment, with high steam imminent—but the kittens were entirely too cute, which meant she ended up playing with them instead.

Of course, that was a mistake, because the next thing Jane knew, she'd fallen in love.

She named the kittens Furry and Catsy and like anyone faced with such adorableness would do, at the end of her shift at the library, she took them home with her.

Which basically meant, they walked upstairs to the apartment above the library.

From that day on, Furry and Catsy accompanied her from home to work and back again.

They went from her apartment over the library, to the town bookstore where she worked part-time in the mornings, and from there, back to the library, this time into the stacks where they played while she helped the occasional patron and read her way through the romance section.

When the library closed around six each evening, they accompanied her back upstairs, where they played and slept and made her apartment a whole lot less lonely.

The kittens appeared a couple weeks before Valentine's Day, so Jane liked to think of them as her Valen-Kitties, and immediately added them to her plans for the day, which were the same plans she made *every* Valentine's Day.

The entire month before the big day, she took advantage of her discount at Zero Books and spent the majority of her paychecks on all the books in the steamy romance section that she hadn't read yet.

This meant she had an entire stack waiting for her to read on V-day.

She'd also purchased a box of brownies and some ice cream, and because they were just so adorable, she bought some catnip toys for the kittens and a plethora of treats for them.

It was hard to resist reading her new acquisitions before the big day, but Jane rarely read new books while working at the library. Instead, she re-read her book donations.

Before Jane took over managing the library, the majority of the collection had been severely outdated since the town council couldn't afford to both pay her salary *and* buy new books.

Once Jane was in charge, though, she started donating every book she purchased—after reading it, of course—to the collection.

She tried to cater to the townspeople's interests by purchasing a variety of genres, including non-fiction (boring!) but mostly—as in almost entirely—she spent her money on romances.

Actually, even her purchases in the other genres usually had *some* romance in them.

Because what was the point of reading a space odyssey if the aliens weren't hot as hell?

Or a thriller if the hero's shirt wasn't going to be torn to shreds in the process of saving the heroine?

Why read an epic fantasy if it didn't include some epic sex? Who wanted to read a thousand pages without a single orgasm on the page, not even one?

No one, that's who.

Jane barely restrained the giggles every time Mr. Higgins, who ran the hardware store, returned one of his thrillers. "They sure don't write 'em like they used to," he'd say.

"But did you enjoy it?" she'd ask.

"Oh, yeah," he'd say with a wink. "Whatcha got for me this week?"

All in all, even though the library really only served eight to ten patrons a week, Jane thoroughly enjoyed her job.

What other job would allow her to read so many

hours of the day while also sharing her love of books with others?

She hosted a book club once a month and every one of those eight to ten patrons attended.

The library (meaning, Jane) provided wine and snacks, which they consumed while discussing the books they'd read the previous month.

It was generally a lengthy list since they rarely read the same books, but they enjoyed a lively debate, arguing over which book deserved the coveted Book of the Month spot in the library.

Usually, at some point, they'd start reading passages from their chosen book, and eventually, as the wine dwindled, those passages would get steamier.

Book club evenings were truly the highlight of Jane's world.

Until the kittens came along.

Now she couldn't wait to introduce Furry and Catsy to her book club members. She just knew they'd be an instant hit.

THE HUMOR LUC FOUND IN THE WOLF'S reaction to his invitation faded upon arrival in Hell, when he discovered his two missing hell-babies hadn't returned in his absence.

It was *infuriating!*

He blamed Merry.

If there was an enchanted doorway in Hell, he had no doubt she was responsible for its existence. She specialized in driving him mad!

It was as aggravating as it was inspiring. She was *definitely* his daughter.

It took him and a full contingent of demons to track down that door and the minute Luc saw it, he knew there'd been some serious shenanigans going on.

There was pixie dust *everywhere,* not to mention the scorch marks on either side of the tiny doorway, evidence two hell-kittens had raked their claws down down the wood, marking their territory.

"Great!" Luc stood, hands on hips, glaring down at the tiny doorway. "We'll be tracking pixies and hell-kittens for days!"

Yaro, one of his best tracking demons, chuckled. "Eh, I only scent two hell-kittens and six, no make that seven, pixies."

"Well, thank goodness for small favors! Just one more pixie and the realms would never recover."

"Sounds kind of fun," Yaro said. "Maybe we should find another pixie."

"Don't you dare!" Luc exclaimed, though he couldn't help but grin. "I mean, sure it'd be a lot of fun, watching all the havoc and chaos, but then you know what would happen."

Yaro made a disgusted noise. "We haven't seen one of *their* kind in eons. Do you really think they'd come back, just because of one wee little pixie?"

"If it were a pixie *we* let loose on the realms?" Luc asked.

Yaro and the other demons nodded. "Hell, yes," they chorused.

"OH, GREAT," BYGUL SAID WHEN THEY POPPED into the library in Zero, Kansas, and saw Jane.

She was sitting behind the front counter, reading a book. One hell-kitten was sleeping in her lap while the other was sprawled on its back across the counter, front paws lifted high, batting at Jane's long, red hair.

Jane held her book in one hand and with the other, was gently petting both kittens, back and forth in long, soothing strokes that had the sound of the cats' purrs filling the library.

"Aw, how cute!" Soraya crooned.

"That's not cute," Bygul said sternly. "It's a disaster waiting to happen or did you forget they're hell-kittens who will grow to the size of horses—"

"Only in their largest forms," Soraya protested.

"—and *she's* entirely, thoroughly, one hundred percent *human.*"

"So?" Soraya asked.

"So non-paranormal humans aren't exactly happy when they realize hell-cats are real," Tivali said.

"Starlight wasn't even fazed a little."

"*Starlight* is the daughter of travelers and as such, grew up wandering the realms," Muezza said. "She's not your typical human."

"I suppose," Soraya said, "but Jane's probably read a million books in her lifetime, which is kind of like visiting a million other realms—well, maybe only a hundred thousand if some of those were series, but still. Maybe she'll surprise us."

"Or maybe we need to replace those hell-kittens for earthbound ones and send these two back to Hell where they belong," Bygul said. "I know we recently matched a bunch, but how many black kittens do we have on our caseload right now?"

Silence.

He glanced around at the other three cats. *"Well?"*

Tivali laid her ears flat and glared at Soraya, who exclaimed, "What? I think it's purrfectly marvelous!"

"What's marvelous?" Bygul asked suspiciously.

"That all the black kittens have been matched. Black cats, too. Our caseload has none left."

"None?" Bygul was incredulous. "How is that even possible? There are *always* black cats and kittens on the caseload."

"You *do* remember the portal, right?" Tivali asked sourly.

"Well, yes, but—hold on. Are you telling me that *all* of our black felines are now roaming the pack lands in Jamesville?"

"They all got matched and not just with the wolves," Soraya said. "The cougars, the witches *and* the fairies chose a few cat companions as well."

"Unbelievable," Bygul said.

"I know! It's a miracle, right?"

"Normally, yes, but right now, no! Now I'm going to have to ask the other matchmaking cats to hook us up with a couple black kittens and they're all going to want to know why and then I'll have to admit that one of our targets built a hell-door." Bygul let out a low growl at the thought of their reactions. "Of course, they'll question what kind of target would *do* such a thing and then I'll have to admit we've been matching the daughters of Satan!"

"Eh, I don't think you're going to get a chance to switch the kittens," Muezza said.

"Why not?"

"Because Lucifer just arrived."

Three

LOVE

THE *ONLY* GOOD thing about this ridiculous, enchanted doorway was that it seemed to lead to just one location.

This meant Luc and his demons would only have to search one realm as they tracked down those wayward pixies. Not to mention his hell-kittens.

The bad news, though, was that the doorway led to earth.

Of course, Luc loved earth. The humans there were so creative and frankly, hilarious. They were true geniuses when it came to all forms of entertainment and Luc traveled there regularly, just for fun.

Unfortunately, the humans also had a bit of a habit of reacting rather hysterically when faced with some-thing they didn't understand, especially if that something happened to be a band of pixies they couldn't see, but could certainly suffer from their mischief.

Now Luc wasn't *blaming* the pixies for the Salem witch trials—after all, the humans came up with that idea all on their own—but the pixies were certainly an instigating factor.

Luc enjoyed a bit of chaos as much as the next demon, but sometimes the end results seemed a bit harsh, as in the case of Salem.

Now that both his daughters were living in the earth realm, Luc would certainly prefer to avoid another inter-realm incident.

An undoubtedly impossible goal, since it seemed he was constantly putting out Hell-spawned fires in one realm or another, and no realm more frequently than earth.

Luc wasn't the only demon in Hell who enjoyed earth realm entertainment.

Braced for almost anything, Luc grabbed one corner of the tiny door, yanked it up so that the door yawned wide, motioned the other demons through, then stepped in himself, before allowing the doorway to collapse back down to its original size.

He found his demons standing in a dark room, but the moment Luc arrived, the room lit up and they found themselves surrounded by shelves of books.

Luc had his own private library, that no one got to see, full of every book he'd been able to find about demons, paranormals, and the known realms of the universe.

This room, he saw, was filled with titles he'd either never heard of or that he'd attempted to purchase, but someone else had beaten him to it.

He scowled.

Merry!

He should have known.

His own daughter, working against him and *worse*, not sharing her finds.

What made it even more infuriating was knowing that the likelihood of Merry sitting still long enough to read even one of these tomes was practically *zero*.

Luc, on the other hand, desperately wanted to explore the stacks of books, but first, he had a couple kittens to find.

Not to mention the pixies.

As it turned out, following the kittens wasn't a difficult task.

They'd left paw marks scorched into the floor that led to the opposite side of the room, where another tiny doorway stood.

Luc scowled.

"We're in a pocket," Lucinda said, making Luc jump.

"Where'd you come from?" He scowled at his twin sister.

She did that all the time.

Just appeared out of nowhere, for no other reason than to aggravate him.

She shrugged. "I've been with you the entire time."

Luc glanced around at the other demons and saw that they looked as thoroughly freaked out as he was.

He *hated* when she did that.

They were twins!

Weren't they supposed to sense where their twin was at all times?

While that seemed to work for Lucinda, who was always popping in at the most inconvenient of moments, *he* never had a clue where she was until she just *appeared* out of nowhere.

"So why are we standing in a pocket between Hell and the earth realm?" She asked with a glint of mischief in her eyes. "And who created this marvelous room full of dark tomes?" She stroked a finger down the spine of a book.

Yaro let out a choked sound.

Luc gave him a sharp look, but the other demon just shook his head.

"Ah. Merry. She always was such a clever child," Lucinda said. "So are we going to visit her?"

Oh, great. If Merry was chaos, then Lucinda was utter bedlam. Put the two of them together and the realms would shudder.

"No," Luc said shortly, hoping she'd lose interest and wander away.

Instead, Lucinda simply raised an eyebrow, glanced around the room at all the other demons, before focusing on Yaro. "Then what *are* we doing?" Her voice was throaty and made every demon, other than Luc, shift on their feet uncomfortably.

Silence as everyone waited to see what Luc was going to do.

Personally, he was all about ignoring that entire situation.

Lucinda had been flirting with Yaro for as long as Luc could remember.

It was like watching a hell-cat toy with its prey.

Yaro stood zero chance of withstanding Lucinda's charms, yet he continued to try.

Luc had no idea why.

"We're tracking down some runaway pixies and a couple missing hell-kittens," Yaro finally answered, clearly unable to withstand Lucinda's intensity a moment longer.

Lucinda whirled and stared at Luc. "You lost your hell-kittens, brother?" Her flirtatious tones morphed to concern in an instant.

"Someone must have stolen them," he growled. "It's possible they left on their own, in search of an adventure, but they'd certainly have returned by now if they could."

Lucinda scowled. "Well, then, let's go teach someone a lesson, shall we?"

Luc silently groaned. Now that Lucinda knew their mission, there was no way she'd abandon them now. No. They were stuck with her for the duration.

It's not that Luc didn't love his sister.

He did.

He'd just been enjoying the peace and quiet as she'd traveled the realms over the last year.

Wreaking havoc elsewhere.

That was always a good thing.

"So are you done traveling then?" he asked.

She shrugged. "For now, at least. I had a bunch of memories return unexpectedly. I didn't even know they were missing. Then, all of a sudden, there they were, taking up an awful lot of brain space. You wouldn't know anything about that, would you?"

"Ah." He should have expected this. "That explanation could take a while."

She sighed. "Fine. Just tell me—is Talon all right?"

"He's more than all right. He's finally happy. He and Starlight are back together."

"That's great. It's weird knowing I forgot she even existed." She fell silent for a moment, then seemed to shake it off with a quick clap of her hands. "So, then, do we know what's on the other side of this door?"

"Nothing more than that it's somewhere in the earth realm."

"Well, let's find out, shall we?" With that, Lucinda reached out and repeated his actions from earlier, pinching a corner of the door and flinging it upward so the door stretched wide enough to allow them all to pass through before it shrank back to its original size.

The other side of the door wasn't much different from the room they'd just exited.

Full of long bookshelves and rows of books.

Though none of those books were as interesting as the ones they'd just left behind.

Therefore, it wasn't the books that brought Luc, his sister and the other demons to a screeching halt.

No, *that* would be the two pixies on top of opposite bookshelves, racing back and forth, sprinkling pixie dust between them.

As the dust sprinkled down, books flew from

shelves, darting across the aisles to shuffle and jostle for new positions on an entirely new bookshelf.

This was going to be a nightmare for whoever took care of these books, especially if they were in any semblance of order before the pixies had arrived.

Shaking his head and leaving his demons to handle the pixies, Luc strode down a different aisle, avoiding the pixie dust entirely—even *he* wasn't immune to its effects—following the fading scorch prints of hell-kitten paws.

JANE WAS ENGROSSED IN A STEAMY HOT SCENE between a city lawyer and a sexy cowboy-vampire, when Catsy leapt to his feet with a happy yowl and launched from the counter.

"There you are, my sweet boy." The raspy growl sent shivers down Jane's spine.

She slowly lifted her head and stared at the two people who stood closer to the stacks on Jane's right than to the front door on her left.

How did these people keep sneaking into the

library without her noticing? Was she losing herself that deeply in her stories?

She was so busy staring at the man, who honestly could have stepped from any one of her favorite romance novels, he was that damn sexy, that it took her a moment to realize Catsy was in his arms, looking a lot bigger than before.

She squinted at the two of them, then glanced down at Furry, who was still napping on her lap, then looked back up.

"What the hell is going on?" She muttered.

Not two minutes ago, the cats were the exact same size.

Now Catsy looked at least three times bigger than Furry. It had to be an illusion or trick of the light. Unless—

"Where's your brother, sweet Chaos?" The man crooned to Catsy.

Damn. Her ovaries might have just exploded.

As if he'd heard her thoughts, the man glanced up and his dark eyes pinned Jane in her place. With a scowl, he strode across the library toward her.

Right before he reached the counter, Furry woke, peeked his head over the counter, let out a happy meow and launched himself from Jane's lap into the waiting man's arms.

This time, Jane was watching and there was no way she could miss the way Furry's body stretched and grew as he soared through the air.

In the time it took Furry to reach the man, Catsy had settled around his shoulders, leaving his arms free to catch Furry on the fly.

Jane was speechless.

Because holy hotness, those large hands stroking up and down Furry's back, not to mention those fingers rubbing his ears, were utterly riveting.

All Jane could think about were those hands roaming her own body and those fingers tweaking sensitive flesh and making her burn.

Just the thought of it sent a wave of heat from the top of her head to the tips of her toes, leaving her shaking and breathless in its wake.

"Well, I see you continue to make an impression, brother."

Jane startled, having completely forgotten about the woman who was standing at the man's side.

She was absolutely beautiful, with wild hair a color that couldn't possibly be natural.

It was red, but not like Jane's hair. Instead, it was brighter and more vibrant, with orange and yellow highlights, all of it working together to create the illusion of a head made of fire. Even the cut of her hair meant the layers and curls flipped in ways that made Jane think of out-of-control flames.

"So you're the one who stole my cats," the man growled, pulling Jane's attention away from the woman's amber eyes. Contacts, Jane suspected, or perhaps just the result of the lighting hitting just right, so that her eyes reflected the colors of her hair.

"*Your* cats?" Jane scowled, then stood and stalked around the counter to face the man, hands on hips. "I'll have you know, *I'm* the one who's been feeding them and taking care of them for the last week and a half. Where have *you* been during that time? Certainly not taking care of *my* cats. Come along, darlings." She made a clicking sound with her teeth that the cats knew meant treats were imminent.

They both immediately launched from the man's arms to hers.

Jane pretended not to notice they shrank a good six inches in the process.

Cuddling the two kittens close, she walked around the counter, set them on top of it, pulled out a bag of treats and started hand-feeding them both.

"You can't just steal my cats," the man growled. "Lucinda, she can't do that."

The woman just chuckled and walked forward to lean against the counter. "They've really taken to you, haven't they? In case you didn't catch it, my name's Lucinda."

"Jane. Nice to meet you. This is Furry." Jane rubbed Furry between his ears, then did the same to Catsy. "And this is Catsy."

"Those *aren't* their names."

"It's nice to meet you, Jane. This is my brother, Lucy."

For some reason, that made Lucy roll his eyes.

Before he could say anything, though, a large crash came from the stacks.

Jane jumped, then raced around the counter and into the stacks, only to skid to a halt when she caught sight of the outrageous disaster waiting there.

Books were *everywhere!*

Worse, standing right in the middle of the entire mess were two, giggling *pixies!*

"You little brats!" Jane exclaimed. "Where have you two been?" She glared at her childhood nemeses. "You both got me in so much trouble back in the day and then you just disappeared. So rude!"

"Janey!" Rebel and Jinx cheered. They leapt into the air and flew across the chaos of books, growing from tiny, six-inch monsters to three-foot ones by the time they reached her.

Throwing their arms around her waist, they rocked her back and forth, crying, "Janey–Baney, we missed you!"

Four

LOVE

"HANG ON. THOSE are pixies!" Bygul exclaimed.

"And the human can *see* them," Tivali marveled.

"How is that even possible?" Bygul demanded.

"I told you Jane might surprise us," Soraya said. "After all, she's read all kinds of paranormal romances. She's probably been prepared for this event for years."

"But she already *knows* the pixies," Muezza said. "I don't understand how that could possibly have happened. Pixies aren't allowed out of Hell."

"Well, it has been known to happen every once in a while," Tivali said. "It's a rare event, though."

"Yeah, because *no one* wants a repeat of the Salem Witch Trials," Bygul said.

"So, how could she have met them?" Muezza asked. "Unless she's been to the Hell Realm before, I don't know how this is even possible."

Bygul growled low in his throat. "I hate mysteries."

"You just don't like it when you don't know everything," Soraya said, shocking Bygul.

Though Soraya could be annoying at times, she was always cheerful and positive, so saying something that could be interpreted as a criticism wasn't exactly typical behavior.

Then again, Bygul had to admit that she was right.

He *hated* not knowing everything.

"Hang on," Yaro said. "The pixies can *talk?*"

Luc snickered and noticed that Lucinda was grinning as well.

"Only to those they like," Lucinda said.

Luc rolled his eyes.

Pixies actually spoke to many people, for many varied reasons.

They'd probably spoken to Jane initially because she'd been their target.

Allowing someone to see and hear them without letting anyone else do the same was just another way of torturing their chosen victim.

The fact that the pixies had hugged Jane, though, told Luc that somehow she'd gone from being just another victim to someone they cared about, and that made Jane very intriguing indeed.

As for allowing other demons to hear them, well, pixies only chose those they believed were as crazy as them for that honor.

This was why Lucinda and Merry had always been able to hear the pixies.

Luc could as well, but he maintained it was only because of the twin-bond with Lucinda that he'd managed such a feat.

No way was he as crazy as even one little pixie.

"Okay, okay, it's great to see you both, but I'm not putting up with your shenanigans in this library, you understand me? Go clean up your mess, right now. I expect every book back in its rightful place in ten minutes. I'll be watching." Jane stood, hands on hips, glaring down at the pixies.

Jinx groaned and Rebel stamped her foot, but Jane was unmoved.

"Now." She pointed over their heads back toward the disaster in the stacks.

Pouting, the two pixies flew back to the scene of their crime, shrinking into their smaller forms as they went. A few moments later, pixie dust and books were flying everywhere.

Jane stood, hands on hips, monitoring the entire process.

Luc watched her, surprisingly fascinated, not even bothering to respond as his demons reported back, one by one, that no other pixies had been found in the library or in the surrounding area.

He was standing with Lucinda on one side and Yaro on the other when Jane reached the end of the aisle she'd been inspecting, turned and said to Jinx and Rebel, who were anxiously waiting her verdict, "Nice job."

The two pixies fluttered up and down, wings beating merrily, and cheered. With each beat of their wings, they grew a little bigger.

As soon as their feet touched the ground, they each grabbed one of Jane's hands and pulled her back down the aisle toward where Luc was waiting.

At the last moment, Jane looked up and Luc could tell by the way her eyes shifted to the left, then the right, then above his head, that she was taking in the entire contingent of demons standing around him.

Luc sent them all a scowl.

When had they dropped their damned glamour? He did a double-take when he realized they *hadn't* dropped it.

He whipped his head back toward the human, who was becoming more and more intriguing with every moment that passed.

"I should have known pixies were just the tip of the iceberg," she said.

"Kitty!" Jinx exclaimed, then leapt for Chaos.

Two things happened immediately.

Chaos lunged forward into his largest form, which for a hell-kitten, wasn't that big at all. At the same time, Jinx shrank to his smallest size and latched onto one of Chaos' ears and the two were off.

Chaos galloped around the room, with Jinx holding on with both hands, whooping and hollering.

Of course, that was entirely too much for Fury, who immediately gave chase, galloping into *his* larger size, with Rebel hurtling after him, swiftly shrinking on the fly. Soon, she too was latched onto her chosen hell-kitten's ear.

"I *knew* they were changing sizes," Jane muttered, "should have known the pixies were involved."

"The pixies have nothing to do with it," Luc said.

Jane glanced at him sharply. "I've *never* known a cat to do that before, including those two, but the minute the pixies arrived, their sizes became fluid. I'd say the ever-changing pixies are definitely the cause."

"Well, then, you'd be wrong," Luc said. "Those cats are *not* from this realm."

That's when it happened.

The human *rolled* her eyes.

At *him.*

Lucifer.

Otherwise known as Satan.

Prince of Darkness.

Lord of the Nine Realms of Hell.

And the Beast.

And those were only the titles he publicly claimed.

Of course, she probably didn't realize exactly who he was. After all, his idiotic sister *had* introduced him by the shortened form of his name.

Perhaps he should enlighten the human.

He opened his mouth to do just that, but she spoke before he could.

"I didn't notice your horns before," she said to Lucinda, "or yours," she said to him. "Were you using a glamour then? Like the Fae?"

"You've met the Fae?" Lucinda asked. "I thought they all retreated an eon ago."

"They did." Luc said. "She must be referring to the fairies."

"Oh, that makes sense," Lucinda said. "Well. More sense than the Fae anyway."

"I'm confused," Jane said.

"So what fairies have you met?" Lucinda asked.

"I'm not aware of any fairies. Unless the pixies count."

"We're *not* fairies," Jinx hollered as Chaos raced by.

"We're pixies!" Rebel shouted as Fury followed his brother.

"You heard them," Jane said with a grin. "They're pixies. So no, I haven't met any fairies."

"You met Merry," Luc pointed out.

"There are several Marys here in town," Jane said, "but I don't know of any Mary fairies."

"Not Mary, M-A-R-Y, *Merry*, as in Merry Christmas."

"Well, in that case, I don't know a Merry at all."

Hm. Well, a library wasn't exactly Merry's typical hang-out place. Then again, she *had* built the doorway there.

Maybe she did it after library hours, though that seemed rather tame for his daughter. Building an inter-realm doorway without the humans noticing would have been just the type of challenge she enjoyed.

"Do you know everyone who stops by the library then?" Lucinda ask.

"Usually," Jane replied. "Though there were a few new faces recently and two of them were women. One was looking for books on the dead—don't ask—and the other a cookbook."

"Merry doesn't like to cook and she's really not much of a reader either," Lucinda observed.

"Was it a chocolate cookbook?" Luc asked suspiciously.

"Why, yes. How did you know?"

He rolled his eyes. So predictable, his daughter. "Well, that was Merry."

"Huh. I never would have expected *her* to be one of the Fae. Then again, she *was* kind of tall."

"She's a *fairy*. It's not the same thing," Luc said.

"And technically, she's only a quarter-fairy," Lucinda said.

"And three-quarters human?" Jane asked.

"Not even close." Lucinda laughed. "Merry and Tempest are both one of a kind."

Luc watched Jane closely when Lucinda laughed, but the human didn't even flinch.

Weird.

Lucinda's laugh was almost as evil as Merry's.

"Tempest? That's right! I completely forgot Tempest's half-sister was visiting." Jane's face lit up as she made the connections. "And that her name is Merry, though I thought it was spelled differently. So, that means you're their aunt Lucinda." She gave Luc a shocked look. "And you're their father?"

"That's right."

"You can't *possibly* be old enough."

Lucinda snickered. "Trust me. He can."

"Huh." A strange look flitted across Jane's face.

If Luc didn't know any better, he'd think it was disappointment.

Jane glanced over her shoulder at the clock on the wall behind her, then faced them once more.

"Well, this has been very interesting, to say the least, but I'm afraid the library is now closed. If you'd like to open a library card and check out some books, I'll certainly stay open long enough for that. Otherwise, I'm going to have to start shutting everything down. Anyone?"

"Uh." The Demons behind Luc all shuffled their feet while grunting and making other awkward sounds of discomfort.

Luc grinned. "I'm afraid most of my companions aren't big readers."

"Well, that's a terrible shame." Jane leaned over the counter, her eyes lit up and she launched into an explanation as to why reading was a glorious pursuit of one's time.

That's exactly how she put it, too, which made Luc chuckle.

As she went on to extol the virtues of reading, Luc was too enchanted by the sound of her voice, the light in her eyes and the way her hair brushed the countertop and swayed as she spoke to really pay attention to the words.

"Don't you think?" she finished brightly.

Luc had no idea what she'd been saying, but the other demons all let out noncommittal grunts, which meant they were too terrified to just walk away.

Funny how a fragile and vulnerable female could wield so much power over the most demonic of males.

"So anyone want to open a library card?"

What followed was the funniest thing Luc had ever seen in his life.

One by one, each and every demon who had accompanied him through the doorway into the earth realm, with the exception of his sister, lined up to fill out applications for a library card.

Luc was curious as to what they were going to use

for proof of address, but he should have known none of them were fazed.

Each produced a wallet similar to the ones he'd seen other humans carrying in this realm, and from inside those wallets, drivers' licenses that actually looked authentic.

Luc might have wandered closer out of pure curiosity, but Jane addressed each demon by name, which meant they'd actually taken the time to ensure their magically produced licenses were technically correct.

He almost laughed out loud when Jane said to Yaro, the first demon in line, "I've never heard of Hell, Kansas before, but then again, I live in a town called Zero, so I shouldn't be surprised."

"Your demons are ridiculous," Lucinda muttered as the two of them stood side-by-side, watching incredulously as demon after demon accepted their library card with a murmured thanks and wandered down the aisles to *actually choose a book*.

This happened because Jane took the time to ask each demon what they would like to read about, something that caused more than one deer-in-the-headlights look from the demons, as they attempted to come up with a suitable, earth realm interest.

Eventually, Jane started giving them options,

which made things go faster. Once she explained that horror was about serial killers and monsters and things that went bump in the night, the rest of the demons all wanted to explore that section.

In fact, Yaro and the first few demons who'd come out of the stacks with books about banal things like cars or computers immediately returned to the stacks, this time to the horror section.

By the time each demon had chosen a book and returned to the line to check it out, the clock behind Jane indicated an entire hour had passed.

The cats and pixies were sound asleep by this time, having completely worn themselves out with all the running and wrestling and playing.

"What about you two?"

"Oh, I'm not much of a reader," Lucinda said. "Neither is Lucy."

Luc gave her a sharp glance and she grinned at him wickedly.

Damn her.

Jane looked absolutely crushed and it was all Lucinda's fault, for making the human think he was an illiterate heathen.

He'd never get a chance with—hold on a minute.

What was he thinking?

A chance? With the human?

"All right, then. Time to go, guys." Jane came around the counter and swept by them, so close that Luc caught her scent as she went by, and the beast inside, the one that had slumbered for half a century now, stretched and lifted its head.

As if a thread connected the two of them, Luc swung around so that he could keep Jane in his sights as she moved across the library toward the front door.

"Follow me now," she said to the demons as she passed them by.

They all fell in step behind her like docile little earth puppies following their mistress.

"What the hell?" Luc muttered.

His Beast let out a low rumble of agreement.

Jane reached the door, held it open and made the process of leaving extraordinarily slow by addressing each and every demon by name as they exited, wishing them a good evening and reminding them to, "Bring your book back when you've finished reading it, so you can choose a new one."

Yaro was the only demon who didn't join the exit line immediately, pausing first at Luc's side to murmur, "Boss?"

"Find the other pixies. I'll round everyone up here."

"Got it." Yaro headed for the door, where Jane waited patiently.

Lucinda snickered. "Yeah, right."

"What?" Luc growled, shifting to the side, so he could keep his eyes on Jane as the last of the demons slowly filed out the door.

"Just that it's not the *pixies* who woke your Beast."

Yaro, who'd finally reached the front of the line and was about to exit himself, froze with one foot still in the library and the other foot on the outside.

Luc's Beast didn't like how close Yaro was standing to Jane and let out a louder rumble than before.

Loud enough the human must have heard because she leaned further out the door to glance up at the sky.

Yaro squared his shoulders and without looking over his shoulder—an act of courage the Beast admired —continued across the threshold.

The Beast didn't settle down when the demon left as Luc had expected. Instead, its eyes were glued to Jane, who still stood partly outside.

Luc was about to go haul her in when she finally stepped back into the library and let the door close behind her. "Why are you two still here?"

Lucinda grinned. "I'm just torturing my brother, that's all." She nudged Luc's shoulder, muttered,

"Good luck," and sauntered past Jane and out of the library.

The minute his sister was gone, Luc could feel his Beast settling, its focus all on Jane.

The two of them couldn't look away as Jane ignored them, bustling around the library, turning off computers, flipping light switches and straightening or relocating the occasional book.

Normally, Luc would expect his Beast to growl or rage at being ignored, but instead, he sensed the Beast was amused.

The most-feared creature in all of Hell was *amused* by a human.

Now he'd seen everything.

"I TOLD YOU!" SORAYA SAID EXCITEDLY. "Didn't I tell you they were purrfect for each other?"

"You're joking, right?" Muezza asked.

"Of course, not. Why?"

"Because the Beast is awake," Tivali said.

"So?"

"So?" Bygul tried to never allow his tail to betray

his emotions, but it whipped around behind him, an obvious sign of his agitation and disbelief that *Soraya*, an actual matchmaking cat of the goddesses, could be so oblivious. "He's the Beast of Hell!"

"I know, but that's not news. We matched both his daughters, including the crazy one. I don't see why we can't match him as well."

"Because he's the *Beast* of *Hell*," Bygul, Tivali and Muezza all exclaimed.

Lucy's attention was focused solely on Jane, to such an extent she felt as if she couldn't breathe.

She wondered if the air conditioner had broken, but then she remembered it was February in Kansas and there was snow on the ground.

Why was it so damn hot in here?

She'd finally finished the closing procedures and had been stalling ever since, grabbing and moving books that didn't need to be moved, to avoid looking at Lucy—a more inappropriate name for the man who watched her so intently, she couldn't imagine—but now there really was nothing more she could do.

She took in a deep breath and faced Lucy, who hadn't really moved the entire time she'd been bustling around the library, except to turn ever so slightly, to always keep her in his line of sight.

She'd never been more aware of a man in her life.

"Well," she said brightly. "That's it for the night." She risked a quick glance at his face and found he'd been waiting for that moment.

Their eyes met and the world faded away.

She couldn't look away as he slowly moved toward her, his eyes holding hers captive.

"They really are amber," she murmured.

"What?"

"Your eyes. And your sister's. They're amber."

He blinked and the redness faded, leaving behind deeply, dark orbs that stared into her soul.

"Jane." His voice was raspy and it sent shivers up and down her spine.

"Yes?"

He leaned forward and buried his nose in her neck.

Jane froze as he took a deep breath in.

Was he *scenting* her?

"What are you?" They both said it at the exact same time.

"What?" Jane pulled away and stared at him. "I'm human, of course. What are *you*?"

"A human who can see through a demon's glamour? Who can see and hear the pixies? Who's been adopted by hell-kittens? Who's caught the attention of The Beast?" He shook his head. "I don't think so."

"Uh. Demons?"

He grinned. "We're all demons, darling. Even non-paranormal humans. They just hide it better. Well, some of them do anyway."

Jane had to admit this was a very good point, though it did nothing to stop the prickling of her scalp, a visceral reaction to the word demon, probably due to her ultra-conservative, religious upbringing.

Of course, the minute she'd turned eighteen, she'd left all that behind, so she had no idea why the word was still triggering for her.

Especially since she didn't believe in any of that.

As far as she was concerned, Hell was just an allegory, as was Heaven.

Probably.

It was the underlying uncertainty that had her hedging her bets, just in case.

She'd always figured if she lived a good life, she'd earn her way to the better place, if it happened to exist.

She wasn't sure talking with a demon qualified her

for that better place, but since he was the sexiest man to walk into the library in, well, *ever*, she wasn't going to let *that* stop her.

"Wait. Did you say hell-kittens?" She whirled and stared across the library at the two kittens, who were currently curled up on the checkout counter, two pixies sprawled on top of them, all four of them sound asleep.

"Yep," he said, "Come along. Time to get these pixies home." He grabbed her hand and dragged her with him toward the counter.

He handed Catsy and Jinx to her, scooped up Furry and Rebel, then slid an arm around her waist and pulled her close so that they stood facing each other, the cats and pixies between them.

He stared into her eyes and for one breathless moment, Jane thought he was going to kiss her, but then the moment passed in a flash of heat and light, and the next thing she knew, they weren't in the library at all.

Five

LOVE

"OH, SHIT," BYGUL said.

Soraya stared down into the library, tail twitching in worry. "What happened? Where'd they go? Where'd he take the kittens?"

"What do you think happened, Soraya?" Tivali exclaimed. "The Beast just kidnapped our librarian."

"But that's marvelous! It proves I was right. They *are* mates."

"Because in all of history, there's never been another reason a demon absconded with a human," Muezza said dryly.

"But we *like* Lucifer. Right? I mean, he's not *that* bad."

"Sure," Tivali said. "Not that bad. Except it's not just Lucifer anymore, is it?"

"The Beast has risen," Muezza said, "and he's already breaking the accords."

"For goddess' sake. That means we have to go back to Hell." Bygul scowled at Soraya. This was all her fault and he was never going to let her forget it. *"Again."*

JANE WHIRLED AROUND IN A CIRCLE, EYES wide. "What? Where are we? What just happened? Where'd the library go?"

She stood in what appeared to be a living room with large leather furniture, a fireplace, huge ceiling fans and walls of windows on all sides.

Outside the windows, a desert landscape that appeared to be intermittently on fire, stretched as far as Jane could see.

Flames erratically burst from the ground, spiraling upward in a huge funnel of fire, only to collapse in on themselves and reappear somewhere else a few moments later.

When they weren't forming cyclones, they were

becoming walls instead, stretching in two directions, dividing and walling off portions of the land, if only temporarily, before sinking back into the ground to be reborn elsewhere.

"Welcome to my home, mate," Lucy said.

Jane jumped and whirled to face him.

"Mrawr." Catsy wrapped himself around her legs, meowing to be picked up.

Jane looked down at him blankly, no memory of having put him down. She leaned down, stroke one hand down his back, then lifted him back into her arms. He purred loudly and Furry came running.

"Mrawr." Furry lifted up on his hind legs and ran his front paws up and down Jane's thighs, a clear sign he wanted to be held as well.

She leaned over and somehow managed to scoop him up without dropping Catsy, the two together becoming a rather hefty armload.

Furry's purr joined Catsy's, so that the entire room sounded like a diesel engine taking off.

Realizing the pixies were no longer hitching rides on the cats, Jane asked. "Where are Jinx and Rebel?"

"Eh, I'm sure they're around here somewhere, making mischief. So tell me, mate," Lucy stared into her eyes, "how did you manage to meet two pixies from Hell anyway?"

"Hell? You mean Hell, Kansas?" She asked nervously, trying not to think about the fact that the flaming desert outside the windows was definitely *not* Kansas.

He grinned. "Well. You can pretend it's Kansas, if you like."

Ugh. That was exactly what she'd been planning to do, but now that he'd said it out loud, she realized that would be like burying her head in the sand and she'd never been one for avoiding reality. With a sigh, she said, "I'd rather know the truth, please."

"As you like."

Jane's heart skipped a beat, for even though his words weren't exactly the same, they were close enough to one of the most romantic phrases in all of rom-com history, to make her swoon a little.

"We're in the Hell realm. There are infinite realms throughout the universe and there are crossings that can be used by those with the knowledge or power."

"So there *is* a realm crossing in my library." How had she worked there for so many years and not had a clue?

"Does a pocket qualify as a crossing? I don't think it does, even though it can be used as such. Besides, that's not how we got here."

"It's not?"

"It wasn't necessary, at least not for me."

What the hell did that mean? "So, you just transported us here? All by yourself? Like some kind of teleporter?"

"Well, the flames of Hell did their part too."

Jane made her way to one of the large leather armchairs and plopped into it, settling Furry and Catsy on her lap.

The two kittens (hell-kittens?) curled around each other and went to sleep.

While they purred and Lucy stood, silently watching, Jane attempted to process everything she'd just learned.

Multiple realms.

A hidden crossing or pocket in the middle of her library.

A pocket she now speculated had been used by the strangers who'd just appeared in the library without seeming to use the actual door.

Strangers who were connected to some of the town's newest residents.

"They're *all* from other realms, aren't they?" she asked faintly.

"Who?"

"The new residents of Zero."

"Actually, no. Well, some of them are. The

vampires relocated to earth about ten years ago, but they're slowly starting to come home, the ones who miss Hell, anyway."

Jane could feel the blood slowly draining from her head.

"And the chameleons have been gone from Hell for a thousand years. I doubt they'll be returning anytime soon. Lot of bad blood there, on account of them being exiled and all."

What the—

"But the witches and the shifters—well, they're all earth humans, so no, they're not from other realms. They're from your own."

"Witches? Shifters? *Vampires?*"

"Oh." Lucy grimaced. "Sorry. Since you can see the pixies, I figured you were like Starlight and already knew about the paranormals in your realm. Guess I was wrong and probably should have eased you into things, huh?"

"Starlight? The waitress from Zero Diner?"

"Former waitress. She's now the manager of Hell's B&B."

Jane would probably want to know more about that later, but she was too busy processing that she was in a realm called Hell, which honestly, was both similar and completely different from what she might have imagined had anyone asked.

Flames? Check.

People screaming and burning in them? Not so much.

That was definitely a relief.

Demons though?

She eyed the man who might qualify as the sexiest man alive if it weren't for the horns and the forked tail. Or perhaps they *solidified* that status. Yeah. Definitely the latter, considering the horns and tail actually intensified his sex appeal.

She'd noticed the tail in the library, but unlike the horns, had thought it would be rude to mention. Now she was wishing she'd given it a bit more thought.

Because demons? Check.

Especially since she just realized what Lucy probably stood for.

Maybe she was wrong though.

She could be wrong.

Maybe Lucy really was his name. It went well with Lucinda.

But then, so did—

"Your real name is Lucifer, isn't it?" She couldn't believe she'd had the courage to ask, but she did and now the question was out there and she had no choice but to wait for the answer.

"It is." Lucifer watched her closely, probably waiting to see if she'd bolt.

Jane was made of sterner stuff, though.

"Why did your sister call you Lucy?"

"She was messing with me. Merry's mate started calling me that—I think it makes him feel better, like I'm less dangerous if he calls me by a shortened version of my name. Honestly, I kind of like it, not that I'll ever tell him that, of course. Or anyone else. Lucinda only called me that because she believed it would annoy me, but since it kept you from panicking, I was fine with it."

Jane let out a scoffing sound. "I wouldn't have panicked."

Lucifer raised an eyebrow.

"It's just a name. I wouldn't have panicked until I arrived *here*."

He left out a bark of laughter.

Okay. She'd processed.

It was a lot to take in, but she was feeling okay about it all.

So she was in Hell.

Big deal.

She'd been to Kansas City a few years back and it

had been way scarier than here. Entirely too many people for someone used to a town of around seventy residents.

Then she'd survived the population boom in Zero, where apparently witches, vampires, shifters and something called chameleons had moved in. And most recently, demons.

Considering all that, visiting Hell wasn't such a big deal.

Not when you considered her childhood best friends were pixies, who used to talk about their home like it was the best playground around.

Not that they'd ever named it Hell, or mentioned the flames, but clearly they loved it here.

And while meeting Lucifer wasn't exactly in her life plans, she was always up for an adventure.

With that in mind, she scooped the cats out of her lap onto the chair beside her, then stood and faced Lucifer, hands on hips. "So why'd you bring me here, anyway?"

As if he'd been waiting for that very question, he immediately prowled closer. "Because, my sweet Jane, you're my fated mate."

Say what now?

"Seriously?" Tivali exclaimed.

"I just don't understand," Soraya said.

"No kidding," Muezza agreed. "You'd think the Lord of the Nine Realms would have a Hell of a lot more game."

"He just blurted it out," Soraya said. "No wooing, no flirting, no passionate kissing, just you're in Hell, let's mate."

"I have no idea why any of you are surprised by this," Bygul said. "Did you miss the part where the Beast is now in charge? Of course, it's got no game. It's been sleeping for fifty years and before that, it was a grouchy hell-monster who everyone tiptoed around because it was so damn horny and cranky."

"Really?" The other cats exclaimed.

"Oh, yeah. It was a true Beast back then. Desperate for its mate after so many millennia alone. That's why it finally went to sleep. It was either that or tear the realms apart looking for a mate who hadn't even been born yet."

"Did it know that?" Tivali asked. "That she wasn't here yet?"

"Probably," Bygul said. "If she'd existed anywhere in the Realms, the Beast would have sensed it and tracked her down in an instant. The only reason Jane made it this far into her lifespan without meeting the Beast is because it was slumbering."

"Well, it's not slumbering now," Muezza said.

"Jane doesn't look too happy," Soraya observed.

"Eh, she's probably just in shock," Muezza said.

"Considering she just learned the Beast is her mate, I think she's doing quite well, actually," Bygul said. "Quite well, indeed."

JANE HAD SPENT HER ENTIRE ADULT LIFETIME reading every book she could get her hands on, and for the last ten years, she'd focused on reading romances—in particular, steamy paranormal ones—so the concept of fated mates wasn't exactly new to her.

That *she* might have one, though—well, that was definitely new.

As was the idea that there were other realms, that her allegory of Hell was an actual place, and that

Lucifer was a flesh-and-blood man, standing in front of her, claiming her as his own.

Holy frack noodles, did that mean she was going to be Satan's Bride?

They'd never even kissed yet. Before she could restrain herself, she blurted out that very thought.

"Don't you think we should kiss first, just to see if we're compatible, before you start throwing scary words like mate around?"

Lucifer's eyes lit up and not in the human way.

Not at all.

Literal flames consumed his pupils, sending a corresponding heat barreling through Jane.

Before she could catch her breath, Lucifer slid into her space, wrapped his arms around her and pulled her close.

"Mate," he growled, then claimed her mouth in a kiss that obliterated every single thought in her head.

Unable to do anything else, Jane kissed him back.

He growled low in his throat, planted one firm hand on her bottom and lifted her higher, so that she could wrap her legs around his hips.

The minute she did, he moved forward until her back hit a wall.

Jane turned her head, just enough to gasp in a deep

breath before diving back into that endless, thorough kiss.

She almost didn't notice when the flames arrived, the scorching, breathless feel of them washing over them both, making her shudder in his arms.

They landed on a bed, soft as silk beneath her.

He settled between her legs, his heavy weight pressing her deeper into the mattress as the flames devoured them whole.

Later, Jane would question whether the flames had been there or not.

Had they really ignited the entire room, burning it to ash, only for it to reform around them, over and over again?

Had the bed beneath them truly burst into flames, a pyre on which they rolled and wrestled and burned?

Did those flames actually lick over their naked flesh without leaving them even a little singed as they came together in a fiery passion that knew no end?

When Lucifer pressed deep, his cock a heated rod that burned in the most exquisite of ways, spreading fire internally, even as she burned on the outside; when she cried out in ecstasy and he roared in answer, did the flames truly jump higher all around them, creating a cocoon of heat and endless desire?

It seemed impossible, yet that very thing kept

happening, again and again, as they spent their passion, rested, then lunged for each other again.

Time passed in that bubble as they loved and burned and loved once more, occasionally dropping into an exhausted sleep, only to wake and burn again.

When the terrible heat and need that had consumed them both finally eased—not entirely, just enough to let them breathe—they woke wrapped in each other's arms, Jane stretched out alongside Lucifer, her cheek over his pounding heart.

His arms were wrapped around her, one hand playing with her hair, the other stroking her back gently.

She lay there and processed what had happened.

Without moving, she tried to take in as much of the room as she could. A fine layer of ash covered *everything,* even the walls.

"We really did burn the room around us," she murmured, her voice a raspy croak.

"Here." Lucifer lifted a hand, flames spurted and a glass of water appeared in his hand. "Drink." He helped her sit up and with one arm wrapped around her waist, gently held the glass for her as she drank.

She'd protest, except her hands shook so badly, she was afraid she'd drop it.

As she reached the end of the water, Lucifer sent the glass away, only to replace it with another.

By the time she was working on the fifth glass of water, she was feeling much better and was able to hold it on her own.

"It won't be this bad next time," Lucifer murmured. "The first time with a mate for my kind is always the roughest. We don't have enough self-preservation to stop, so we tend to go until the heat finally subsides, at which point, we usually find ourselves a dehydrated mess."

Jane glanced at him. "You're not drinking?"

"I will when you've had your fill."

Jane's heart melted a little because he could have chosen to fetch a drink for himself at the same time, but then he'd have had to stop supporting her in order to hold his own glass.

When she finally stopped drinking, he raised an eyebrow, but she shook her head. "I'm good."

He nodded, sent her glass away for the last time and fetched a full one for himself.

"That's a pretty handy trick."

He gave her a questioning look while downing the first glass of water.

"The flames."

"Ah, yes." He finished his glass of water and

replaced it with a new one. "Not every demon of my kind can do it, but some can."

"What kind of demon, are you?"

"Can't you guess?"

"Devil."

"Exactly."

"So Lucinda?"

"Also a devil."

"Tempest and Merry?"

"Half-devils. Tempest's mother is a witch and Merry's mom is half-witch, half-fairy."

"Do they both have the tail and horns?"

"Tempest has the tail, but no horns. Merry didn't get either. Instead, she received fairy wings from her mother. Not that either girl appreciates their extra appendages. They tend to hide them, no matter what realm they're in, including Hell. It makes sense in Merry's case, considering even the fiercest of creatures are a little scared of the fairies, but Tempest should be proud of her tail. Instead, she hides it."

Jane nodded, then asked abruptly, "So we're fated mates then?"

Six

"WE ARE," Luc said. He felt a huge blast of relief that Jane was finally addressing the fiery elephant in the room.

He hadn't wanted to bring it up himself, in case she wasn't ready. He'd wanted to give her time to process, but he was already over that. If she hadn't said something, he'd have interrupted her processing time to force the matter.

Thankfully, the intensity of their coming together had sent his Beast back to sleep because it would never have allowed her even that much processing time. Instead, it probably would have claimed her again, the minute she woke.

Luc had no illusions the Beast would sleep for long, though.

Now that they had claimed their mate, it would be popping back in on a very regular basis.

"So what exactly does that mean?" Jane asked.

"Well—"

Before he could answer, though, the sound of his front door opening caught his attention.

Luc scowled. "Who the hell—"

"Dad!"

Jane's eyes widened. "Is that—"

"Merry," he growled.

"We're here," another voice shouted.

"And is that—"

"Tempest." Seriously, his daughters had the worst timing in all the realms. Not even the archangel Gabriel was this bad.

"Hey, Uncle Luc! Merry said it was okay for us to crash this party."

"And that's Talon, which means he's probably got his mate with him."

"Yo, Lassiter. Where's that brother of ours anyway?"

Jane grinned, obviously recognizing Lucinda's voice. "Is your entire family planning to join us for dinner?"

That's when it clicked for Luc. "Hellfire and

damnation. It's the monthly family dinner. And I haven't even started cooking."

"You cook?"

"Upon occasion."

"Nice." The look on Jane's face told Luc that having a devil-mate who cooks was a pleasant surprise. "We should probably go downstairs, don't you think? Before they decide to hunt you down."

Luc groaned. "Fine. Let's get dressed." He stood and lifted Jane from the bed, taking advantage of the moment to kiss her thoroughly.

They were both breathless when he pulled back.

"I don't have any clothes," Jane said. "They either burned or were shredded or both."

"Eh, no worries."

Flames erupted in the center of the bed and when they died down, a couple pairs of jeans and t-shirts were waiting there.

Jane grinned. "Like I said, a *very* handy trick."

"WHO INVITED THE FAMILY?" SORAYA

exclaimed. "They were about to have *the* conversation!"

"Didn't you hear him?" Bygul asked. "Lucifer did."

"Well, this is just epically bad timing," Tivali snapped.

"The worst," Muezza agreed mournfully.

"Maybe we should go track him down," Tempest said. "It's not like him not to have dinner already on the table."

Merry looked at Talon and the two of them rolled their eyes in unison. As if her father couldn't handle himself.

"He hasn't even started cooking," Tempest fretted.

"Eh, I'm sure he's fine," Matthew said.

"Bummer," Sam muttered.

Merry snickered. "Do you think you'll ever *not* be intimidated by my father?"

Sam glared at her. "He's a scary dude, Merry. So are you, to be honest, but at least you're my mate. You have a reason not to kill me. He's got none. In fact, he's probably come up with a hundred thousand reasons to take me out."

"Oh, it's a least two hundred thousand," Merry's father said as he strolled into the room, a woman at his side.

Merry narrowed her eyes.

Hold on. She knew that woman.

"You're the Zero librarian!"

She smiled at Merry. "I am. My name's Jane." She held out her hand, but there was nothing in it, not even one tiny morsel of chocolate, so Merry ignored it.

"I'm Sam." He leaned over and shook the librarian's hand. "This is Merry. We're mates."

"It's very nice to meet you both."

"What are you doing here?" Merry asked abruptly. "In Hell? With my father?"

"Merry," Her father said her name in a warning tone of voice.

"What? I'm just curious. That doorway was pixie-sized, so there's no way a human would have found it *or* made it through." Merry narrowed her eyes at her father. "She had to have had help because there aren't any realm crossings in Zero, Kansas."

"You're right," Jane said. "Your father made that happen."

Weird. Her father had never shown any interest in

humans before, so why was he transporting one to Hell now?

"Jane, it's so lovely to see you." Talon's mate, Starlight, stepped forward and hugged Jane.

"You too, Starlight. I'm afraid I haven't been anywhere but the library and bookstore for a while, so I didn't realize you'd relocated. You're no longer waitressing at the diner?"

"That's right. I had a wonderful opportunity here and, well, I had to take it."

"Jane!" Jasmine ran into the room and flung her arms around Jane's waist.

"Well, hello, Jasmine. I haven't seen you in the bookstore in quite some time."

"That's because we moved to Hell and we found my daddy and I got hell-kitties for Christmas! Don't worry, though. The B&B hooked me up. There weren't any books when we moved in, on account of Hell not having any, but then once the B&B knew what we wanted, it created an entire library for me and my mommy."

"Hang on. There are no books in Hell?" The librarian looked horrified, but Merry's father hurried to reassure her.

"Of *course*, there are."

Merry couldn't believe it, but her father looked a

bit worried. Did he actually *care* about the human's feelings?

Merry stared, incredulously, as her father slipped an arm around the librarian's shoulders and whispered something in her ear.

That's when it dawned on Merry that it wasn't just caring. He actually wanted the human to *like* him, maybe even admire him!

Satan.

Worried about a human's opinion.

How was this even *possible*?

Had the librarian somehow bewitched the literal Lord of the Nine Realms?

Before Merry could reach a conclusion about her father's bewitched status, he said, "Why don't we all go into the dining room and sit down? I'm sure dinner's ready by now."

The librarian gave him a startled look. "You haven't even started cooking it yet."

He grinned and steered her toward the dining room. "Cooking isn't really necessary when you're me."

Merry rolled her eyes.

"Ugh. His ego gets bigger every year," her uncle Lassiter muttered.

Tempest just giggled and led the rest of them into

the dining room, where they all saw that indeed, dinner had been served.

The librarian looked stunned from where she stood at one end of the table, staring at the food, mouth agape.

She then seemed to recover and settled into the chair to the right of the head of the table.

A chair Merry's father was holding for her.

What the ever-loving Hell was going on?

Once everyone else was seated, her father tapped a spoon against his glass.

Weird. Was he going to make a speech?

"My dear family, I am so happy to have all of you here today."

He was!

He was *actually* making a speech right now!

"We're still celebrating Starlight and Talon finding their way back to each other, and in the process, bringing Jasmine into the fold." He paused as everyone clapped and offered congratulations, or in Jasmine's case, bounced up and down in her chair and cheered.

"And of course, my very own daughters, for finding their mates in the earth realm of all places. Merry is here with her wolfy mate, what's-his-name." He waved a hand as if it was of no importance, making Merry snicker and Sam bristle.

"Even more shockingly, we have one of the Exiled at our table tonight, perhaps the first time one has ventured back to Hell in a thousand years. Welcome, Tempest's mate."

Merry sensed Sam subside a bit, as he realized her father couldn't be bothered to learn the name of her sister's mate either.

Though entertaining, Merry had no idea where this stupid speech was going, and that bothered her greatly.

"We have one more thing to celebrate this evening and that is Jane." He held out a hand to the librarian —*why* they were celebrating a human, Merry couldn't imagine.

The librarian placed her hand in his and allowed him to pull her to a standing position.

He again slid an arm around her, this time pulling her into his space, so that she stood with her back to his chest and his arms wrapped around her from behind.

The light finally dawned for Merry, but she simply couldn't believe it.

No way would the Fates have chosen to pair the Beast of Hell with—

"Family. May I present to you, my fated mate, Jane."

"Janey! Yay, Janey!" Two pixies zipped around the dining room, lightning fast, sprinkling pixie dust everywhere before landing on the librarian's shoulders, one on each side.

Merry straightened in her chair and looked at the human with new eyes.

How in the Hell had a human librarian caught the attention of these two pixies?

She then had to look away, gagging, because her father decided to sweep his mate over his arm and kiss her senseless.

Gross!

"Uh, what exactly are those pixies doing?" Matthew asked.

Merry really didn't want to look, but she took a quick glance and blanched. Oh, great.

The stupid pixies were hovering above her father and Jane, merrily sprinkling dust over the two of them.

Merry looked closer.

Crap.

A quick glance showed the entire table was covered in pixie dust, as were the people seated at it.

The only difference was the color of the dust.

Lassiter and Jasmine were the only ones who'd been dusted in silver.

The rest of them, though.

She had a moment to wonder if the effects might not be as potent as she'd always heard, before a searing wave of heat barreled over her in a rush of need.

Shit.

She stood quickly. "This dinner's over. Everyone go home before we all get an eyeful that none of us want."

"What are you talking about?" Tempest asked distractedly, as she climbed from her chair to straddle Matthew in his.

"We've been pixie dusted in *Red*," Merry said.

Lassiter and Talon both lunged to their feet.

Lassiter scooped Jasmine into his arms, announced to the room, "I've got Jasmine," then left the room so fast, he was a blur.

Merry imagined in normal circumstances, Starlight would have demanded to know where he was taking his granddaughter and why he was leaving so quickly, but these weren't normal circumstances.

Talon already had Starlight in his arms, and was busy kissing her, even as he raced from the room just as quickly as his father had.

Meanwhile, Tempest was kissing Matthew and their father had already disappeared in a rush of flames with Jane in his arms.

Merry decided Tempest and Matthew could have

the dining room—though they might have to burn the table afterwards—and hauled Sam out of her father's house.

The moment the door closed behind them, Sam flung back his head and howled at the moon.

Merry rolled her eyes.

Earth wolves.

So damn goofy.

The heat was becoming unbearable, which meant she needed a location to take him soon.

Like *now*.

Unfortunately, Talon would have taken Starlight to the B&B, so they couldn't go there, and Lassiter was probably at the Vampire compound with Jasmine right now, so that was out.

In fact, if Lassiter had gotten hit by even a tiny bit of Red, he would leave Jasmine under the care of the Coven to head to the nearest bar, to pick up some poor innocent bystander, who would undoubtedly never recover from a pixie-induced lusting.

This meant avoiding all motels and hotels in the vicinity of any bar.

Damn.

She'd just go back inside her father's house, but between Tempest and her mate in the dining room and their father and his mate in his bedroom, Merry wanted nothing to do with that option.

That's when her eyes lit on the treehouse.

Sure it was surrounded by hellfire, but that just made it all the more challenging.

She went to grab Sam's arm, only to miss because he was busy shifting.

Lunging forward, she caught his wolf just as he was about to run off into the desert and lifting him, flung him over her shoulder and set off for the treehouse.

This was actually much better.

She could run the gauntlet of fire like always, and by carrying her mate, she could be assured he wouldn't actually burn to death in the flames of Hell.

JANE WOKE, FEELING AS IF SHE'D BEEN drinking all night long and was now dealing with the aftereffects.

"What the hell?" she groaned, not even lifting her head from where it rested on Lucifer's chest. "Why am I so hungover?"

"Pixie dust hangover," Lucifer muttered. Unlike the day before, his hands weren't roaming and stroking her body. Instead, he held the two of them perfectly still, making Jane think he might also be feeling poorly.

"Jinx and Rebel have always sprinkled dust everywhere. I've never had this reaction before," Jane protested as softly as she could, in an attempt to keep her head from exploding.

"It's because they used Red on us."

"Red?"

"Also known as LD, Red costs a fortune because it's so rare."

"Why would anyone want a dust that makes them feel so awful the next day?"

"Because it's not about what happens the next day. It's about the night before."

At that statement, memories blazed through Jane's head. Heat poured over her in a rush as she remembered the lust-filled hours of the night. "LD. Lust Dust?"

"Yep."

"I might kill them. If I ever manage to gain my feet again."

Lucifer chuckled. "Don't worry. The aftereffects will wear off in about fifteen minutes. They don't last long, which is why most people find Red to be worth it."

"WHO KNEW RED PIXIE DUST WAS THAT potent?" Tivali exclaimed.

"I certainly didn't," Muezza said.

"I wonder if the pixies would be willing to donate some for the cause," Soraya said.

"What cause?" Muezza asked.

"The matchmaking cause, of course."

Bygul stared at her incredulously, gratified to notice Tivali and Muezza were doing the same.

"What?" Soraya asked.

"The pixies only use the dust on mated pairs," Bygul said. "It wouldn't be right to use it otherwise."

"But Lassiter wasn't mated," Soraya said.

"Which is why the pixies dusted him and Jasmine in silver," Tivali said. "It's also why he took her with him—because no little girl needs to see where that scene was headed."

"Huh. Well that's disappointing," Soraya said.

"Why's that?" Muezza asked.

"I was hoping to use the pixie dust to make some matches," Soraya said, "but if we can't use it on unmated humans, well, that's just not very helpful."

"Because it would be *wrong,*" Tivali said severely.

Seven

"I'M STARVING," JANE announced, not bothering to lift her head from Lucifer's chest. She was quite comfortable right where she was.

"Hmm," he murmured in agreement.

Jane had no idea how much time passed while they lay in each other's arms, ignoring their grumbling tummies, but eventually the sound of the front door opening reached their ears.

"Again?" Lucifer growled.

"Dad," Merry's voice shouted from below. "Family dinner just became family breakfast! I'm on kitchen detail, but you'd better get moving because everyone's on their way!"

Lucifer jackknifed to a sitting position, dragging Jane with him.

"What? Why?" Jane shoved her hair out of her face and glared at her mate—her *mate!* She could feel the glare melting right off her face as the wonder of having a fated mate, even a demonic one, washed over her.

"I need to get down there or we'll all be having chocolate for breakfast," Lucifer said.

"Like chocolate chip pancakes? That doesn't sound so bad."

"Like chocolate syrup on cereal since Merry doesn't cook."

"Well, in theory, chocolate should make everything better, so maybe it's the new breakfast combination no one's discovered yet."

"Oh, Merry's discovered it and if we're not quick enough, she'll be demanding everyone try it."

Jane giggled. "So I guess we're getting dressed then."

"Unfortunately." Lucifer sighed.

Almost an hour later, after a lengthy shower they took together "to save time," Jane followed Lucifer into the kitchen, where they found Tempest and Matthew cooking side-by-side, Sam digging in the fridge, setting ingredients on the countertop, and Merry sitting on a bar stool at the island, eating what appeared to be chocolate covered candies, arguing about how to best serve eggs.

"You're putting chocolate syrup on them, right?" Merry demanded.

"Gross," Tempest said. "I love chocolate as much as the next witch, but who would want it on eggs?"

"I would," Merry said. "Anyone with taste would. Chocolate makes *everything* better."

"I can attest that it most certainly does *not,*" Sam said. "Chocolate on broccoli is purely disgusting."

"That's only because you hate broccoli," Merry said.

"Nasty little trees," Sam muttered, "but somehow they're *worse* dipped in chocolate."

"Not true," Merry said. "They're infinitely better."

"They looked like a plateful of turds," Sam said, "and they tasted worse."

"Eaten some turds in your time, have you?" Lucifer asked, catching everyone's attention.

"Dad!" Merry exclaimed. "About time you got down here. Come have the chocolate breakfast of champions."

Jane giggled, then whispered to Lucifer, "Is Merry pregnant? Is she having cravings?"

Lucifer let out a bark of laughter. "Nope. That's just Merry being Merry."

Interesting.

"Janey!" Rebel and Jinx came flying into the room, followed by Jasmine and Lassiter.

The two pixies landed on Jane's shoulders, hitching a ride as they used to when she was a child, while Jasmine made a beeline for Merry, who helped her onto a stool and graciously slid her bowl of chocolate candies toward the little girl.

"Yay!" Jasmine crowed, scooping up a handful of chocolate.

Jane winced, wondering if any of the adults in the room were going to stop the child from eating her weight in chocolate for breakfast.

No one seemed so inclined, a fact Jane was certain they would all regret later.

At that moment, Starlight and Talon arrived, bustling into the room with huge smiles on their faces.

Actually, as Jane looked around, she realized that everyone seemed pretty happy and relaxed.

Even Lassiter, who'd been on babysitting duty last night, something Jasmine enjoyed sharing about in between bites of chocolate.

"It was the best sleepover ever, Mom! I got to hang out with the vampires. We watched Disney movies and we did our hair and painted our nails—look!" She held out her hands and everyone admired the colorful paint jobs.

"Wow, someone's really talented at nail art," Jane said.

"It was Aunt Dinara," Jasmine said. "She's an artist. Blade wasn't too bad either. Pops was the worst though."

"Hey!" Lassiter exclaimed.

Jasmine giggled. "Sorry, Pops, but it's true. It took Dinara forever to get rid of the mess on my nails so she could fix them after you got done with them."

"But we had fun, right?" he asked with a grin.

"The best!"

"Hey, fam, I'm here!"

"Dinara!" Jasmine cheered, adding another cheer, when Dinara arrived in the kitchen with company. "Lucinda!"

Lucifer let out a groan. "We'll never get rid of them now."

Those words proved prophetic.

Tempest and Matthew announced that breakfast was ready, so there was a mad scramble as everyone helped carry the food into the dining room.

In minutes, they were all seated at the dining room table, passing bowls and platters piled high with eggs, sausage, bacon, potatoes, pancakes, pastries and more.

What followed was a truly chaotic breakfast meal, the likes of which Jane had never experienced in her life.

They ate and laughed, shared stories and teased one another, and the room rang with laughter and joy.

Rebel and Jinx settled into their larger forms and sat on either side of Jasmine, the three of them giggling together like little children.

Watching them, Jane had a moment of true nostalgia for her childhood years, full of innocence, when her best friends were two pixies no one else could see.

"So when are you going to share the story of how you met these two trouble-makers?" Lucifer asked Jane when the came a lull in the conversation around them.

Jane shrugged. "There's not much to tell. They were around my entire childhood."

"So, you grew up here in Hell, then?" Talon asked.

"What? No. In Iowa."

"That's not possible," Lucifer said. "The pixies aren't allowed out of Hell."

"Pixies do what pixies want," Jinx said. "We may be small, but we can't be controlled."

"Jinx!" Rebel hissed.

"Hang on," Talon exclaimed. "Are you saying

pixies haven't been confined to Hell like we all believed?"

The two pixies looked at each other, then seemed to come to a conclusion.

"Vampires aren't confined," Jinx said.

"Chameleons left a thousand years ago," Rebel said.

"Devils travel the realms whenever they want, without a crossing," Jinx said.

"So, why should pixies be any different?" Jinx asked.

"Because pixies cause trouble wherever they go!" Lucifer exclaimed.

"Devils unleashed the flames of Hell in the Ice Realm just last week," Rebel snapped.

"Two Incubi caused a riot in Las Vegas last month," Jinx said.

"A harpy went on a rampage in the troll realm two weeks ago," Rebel said.

"A gorgon—" Jinx began.

"All right, all right. You've made your point," Lucifer said. "So what you're telling me is that pixies have somehow figured out their own way out of Hell and you've been wreaking havoc across the realms without any oversight for centuries."

"Well, maybe only a few decades," Jinx said. "And mostly, it's just been Rebel and me."

"Why'd you stop visiting?" Jane asked.

"We didn't," Rebel said sadly. "One day, you just woke up and you couldn't see or hear us anymore."

"Really?"

"We missed you."

"Puberty," Lucinda announced.

"What?" Jane, along with everyone else at the table, stared at her in confusion.

"It's especially potent among earth humans. All those hormones going crazy. Sometimes it causes them to see what they could never see before and sometimes it does the opposite."

"Well, that sucks," Jane said. "What reversed it?"

"Mrawr." Furry jumped onto Jane's lap, bumped his head under her chin and starting making biscuits on her thighs.

She hissed at the prick of his claws, but started petting him gently. "Hello, my sweet, little Valen-kitty. Where's your brother, baby?"

"Mrawr." Catsy leapt onto her lap as well, but only long enough to snatch a piece of bacon off her plate, before leaping down to the floor where he proceeded to eat his prize.

Jane giggled.

"And there's your answer," Lucinda said as Furry apparently came to the conclusion that he was missing out, whirled toward the table and snatched his own piece of bacon.

Unlike Catsy, though, Furry hunkered down on Jane's lap and starting eating his prize right there.

"My guess is Fury and Chaos did something that sparked that dormant part of your brain back to life," Lucinda said.

"Are you talking about Furry and Catsy?" Jane asked.

"Those are ridiculous names," Lucifer said, "and certainly not menacing enough for a couple hell-kittens who will grow into fierce creatures."

"I'll have you know their names are perfect, especially for two adorable Valen-Cats," Jane said. "Beside, those are only their nicknames. Furry is short for Furlock Holmes, an absolutely brilliant detective, and Catsy is short for Dr. Catson, his wonderful associate."

Lucifer just stared at Jane, an incredulous look on his face.

"What? They're truly fantastic names!"

"You named the hell-kittens after two *fictional* characters?" he exclaimed.

Jane beamed at him, delighted that he recognized

the names. "Of course, I did. They're absolute masterpieces, both the books *and* the kittens."

"Huh." He let out a grunt she couldn't quite interpret, then said, "Well, I suppose that's fine, but I'll continue to call them Fury and Chaos."

Jane rolled her eyes, but secretly, she was amazed at how similar their names were.

"Anyway," Lucinda drawled, "as I was saying. Some subconscious part of you Jane, undoubtedly recognized the kittens weren't regular cats and everything started coming back. For that matter, you'd already met Merry, plus Zero, Kansas is a hotbed of paranormal activity lately, so you've probably been on the verge of being able to see through glamour for quite some time. The kittens, the pixies and finally, the arrival of your fated mate just made it all inevitable."

"I have a question," Merry spoke up. "Are you *certain* she's your fated mate, Dad? I mean, look at her. She's completely, irrevocably, helplessly human."

"Hey!" Jane exclaimed.

"Janey's not helpless," Jinx said.

"Though she *is* human," Rebel said.

"Yes, which brings me to my next question," Lucifer said. "But first, yes, Merry, I'm certain she's my mate. As for you two." He glared at the pixies. "Since when do pixies make friends with non-paranormal earth humans?"

"Since Janey started telling us stories," Jinx said.

"She knows the best stories," Rebel said. "She used to read to us every day."

"Plus, she taught us how, so we could read on our own whenever we wanted."

"Interesting."

"I did teach you guys to read." Jane grinned. "I think you were the first ones I ever taught. The first ones I talked to about my favorite books, too. You should come to my Book Club. It's—" Jane froze, horrified. She hadn't even given a single thought to either one of her jobs since discovering Lucifer was her mate. "What day is it today?"

"Well, we don't exactly count the days here, since it never really gets dark," Lucifer said, "but it's Saturday in the earth realm."

"*Saturday?*" But Valentine's Day was Saturday. She was supposed to spend the day reading her giant stack of steamy books, then lead a Book Club tonight. Then again, living out her own, steamy romance was turning out way better than spending the day reading. Still—"I haven't been to either one of my jobs in three days."

"Don't worry about it," Lucinda said. "I left a note

on the library door, saying the library was closed for renovation."

"Renovation?" Jane exclaimed. "That's a terrible excuse! People will expect to see actual improvements when the library reopens. I don't have the funds to renovate!"

"Don't worry," Lucinda said cheerfully. "Renovations are in progress as we speak."

"What kind of renovations? Did you get approval from the Town Council? Do you have all the necessary permits?"

"Permits?"

Jane groaned. "I'm going to lose my job. Which means I'm going to lose my home because it comes with my job."

"Your home is now with me," Lucifer growled.

She waved a hand in dismissal. "Not the point."

LUC SCOWLED. OF COURSE, IT WAS THE POINT! "You don't need to worry about the library either. It's not like you need the job anymore."

Jane gasped, then glared at him.

He reared back, shocked that she would give *him* such a fierce look. After all, he was her beloved mate. "What?"

"I don't work at the library because I need a job!" She didn't?

"I don't work at the bookstore because I need one either. If I wanted to get a job I *need*, I could work anywhere. I work at the library and the bookstore because I love *books*. And it doesn't matter what changes happen in my life, I'm not living anywhere, or working any job that doesn't involve *books*."

That wasn't good news.

Luc had always thought when he found his mate, she'd quit her job and rule Hell with him.

"But there aren't any books in Hell," Jinx said.

What the Hell? "Yes, there are," Luc snarled. "Stop saying that! You'll make her hate it here."

"But it's true," Rebel said. "Why do think we go to Earth so often? Because they have the best books!"

'We have books in Hell," Luc said emphatically. He glared around the table, infuriated to see doubtful looks on *everyone's* faces. Worse, his daughters were giving him pitying looks and his brother and sister simply looked at him like he was mad. Where was the loyalty? "We do," he assured Jane.

Jane didn't look as if she believed him though. In

fact, she looked as if she trusted the pixies' word more than his. Again, where was the loyalty?

"What *kinds* of books?" she asked suspiciously.

"What do you mean? All kinds of books."

"*Not* all kinds," Rebel contradicted him.

"There are *plenty* of very interesting books in Hell," Luc said.

Lucinda made a face, one that told him he was stretching the truth a bit.

Well, she hadn't read any of the books he'd gathered over the years, so she wouldn't know!

They *were* very interesting.

Many came from *other* realms, of course, but some came from Hell.

A few.

Okay. Maybe one or—

One.

Written by him.

But still. Just because he didn't have many—or any—in his own private collection didn't mean there weren't any books in Hell.

He just had to convince Jane of that.

"There are so many popular books here."

Lassiter shaking his head toward the other end of the table broke Luc's concentration for a moment, but then Jane raised an eyebrow at him, clearly wanting more information, so he went right back to convincing her.

"Some were written by the greatest minds in all the realms. In fact, I'm sure they would be award-winning books, you know, if Hell had awards for books and things. Plus bestseller lists! If we had those types of lists, they'd definitely be on them. Because they're wonderful and very well-written and extremely well regarded and—" Aggravated that no one seemed convinced, he ended with a shouted, "*We have books here!*"

"Does anyone else think Lucifer's perhaps protesting a bit too much?" Muezza asked.

"Oh, he's definitely protesting too much," Tivali said.

"Yeah, well, that's because the pixies are right," Bygul said. "Hell may have books, but they're all educational in nature. You know. Non-fiction."

"Wait. There's no fiction anywhere in Hell?" Tivali demanded.

"Well, not unless Lucifer has some in his private collection."

"This is terrible," Soraya wailed. "Why didn't you tell me? I thought this was the purrfect match, but it turns out it's a nightmare!"

"I'm pretty sure I said in the very beginning this was a bad idea," Bygul said.

"And I said it would be a match made in Hell," Muezza said. "So it turns out we were right. This match is doomed."

LUC SEALED HIS MOUTH SHUT AFTER THAT last outburst, determined not to say another word. He couldn't *believe* that she had him rambling—him! Lord of the Nine Realms of Hell. Rambling!

"Hmm." Jane stared at him, then looked across the table at the pixies, who shook their heads, sorrowful looks on their faces.

Impudent little bastards.

Luc dragged a finger across his neck and pointed at the two pixies, who finally looked a little concerned.

"Well, there *are* books," Jinx finally allowed. "Demon schools are *full* of books."

"Boring books," Rebel muttered.

"What about the libraries?" Jane asked.

Oh, shit. Before Luc could come up with a distraction, Jasmine let the hell-cat out of the bag.

"Hell doesn't have any libraries," she said.

"No libraries?"

The pixies and Jasmine all shook their heads.

"What about the book stores?"

"There aren't any of those either," Jinx said.

"But how do the schools get books if there aren't any book stores?"

"They just order them from the warehouse," Rebel said.

"Right." Jane glared at Luc. "I'm not living anywhere that doesn't have libraries or bookstores. I'm also not giving up my jobs on earth."

"But I have my own library," Luc blurted out, in an admittedly desperate attempt to salvage the situation.

"You do?"

"Of course, I do. I love books."

"Now that is true," Lucinda said. "In fact, Luc's a bit of a nerd in that regard."

"OH, THANK GOODNESS." SORAYA PLOPPED onto the ground and closed her eyes. "I was getting worried there for a minute."

"I don't know why you're so relieved," Bygul growled. "The chances of the Beast having steamy, paranormal romances in his collection are slim to none."

"I hate to say it, but I have to agree with Bygul," Tivali said. "I don't think we're out of the woods yet."

"Oh, that's okay. Jane reads all kinds of genres. So even though she prefers romance, she's be okay reading other genres like adventure or mystery or science fiction. As long as there's some fiction available, we should be okay."

WELL, THANK GOODNESS.

Jane had been getting a bit worried there for a

moment, thinking the fates had steered her wrong, to match her with someone entirely wrong for her.

"Okay, so what genres are we talking about?"

"Genres?"

"Paranormal romance?" She asked hopefully.

He shook his head.

"Yeah, that was probably too much to ask for. Any romance at all?"

"Afraid not."

"Mysteries?"

"No."

"Fantasy?"

"No."

Jane narrowed her eyes. "Science fiction?"

Luc shook his head.

"Hold on. Do you have fiction in this library of yours?"

He winced. "Well, you see, the books I mentioned?"

"The ones that would win awards and land on bestseller lists?"

"Yeah, those."

"Uh-huh."

"They'd all be for the non-fiction awards and best-seller lists."

"Seriously? The only books in Hell are non-fiction?"

"You'd be surprised how many realms only produce non-fiction. Only they don't call it non-fiction, they just call it history or science or geography or whatever."

"I'm so disappointed right now."

"Don't worry, Jane, the B&B gives me any books I want. You just tell me what you want and I'll make sure the B&B gets it for you."

"Thank you, Jasmine. That's very sweet of you, but I think I'll just keep my jobs on earth and get my own books."

At that moment, the sound of the front door opening reached their ears and a few seconds later, Yaro came stomping inside the dining room.

He had five pixies riding his shoulders, two on one side, three on the other. The rest of the demons who had opened library cards earlier that week followed.

"We tracked down the rest of the pixies," Yaro reported. "They were torturing the local wolf pack."

Luc snickered.

"Did you just return from Zero, Kansas?" Jane demanded.

Yaro nodded.

"What time was it there?"

"Just after one."

Jane leapt to her feet. "Well, I don't care what's going on in the library. I've got a Book Club at five and I'm not canceling it, so you need to figure it out, Lucifer. Get me back to my library so I can get set up."

"What's a book club?" Yaro asked.

Eight

MERRY TUNED OUT the rest of the conversation because who cared about books?

Besides, she was still stuck on the fact that her dad's fated mate was a human librarian.

The more she thought about it, the more intriguing it became.

Not just because he and the librarian were both into books, in a totally nerdy way.

No, it was more than that.

It was the fact that Merry had created a pocket library for her father as a gift and somehow when he'd found it, it had led him to his fated mate.

What were the chances of that?

Sure, she'd anchored the pocket to the library in

Zero, Kansas, but that was just because it made sense. After all, Tempest lived in town and it would give him an excuse to visit her often.

When Merry chose that location, she'd had no idea the librarian working there would end up becoming her father's fated mate.

That was some truly powerful magic at work there.

And not witchy magic.

"Fate magic," she muttered to Sam.

"What's that?"

"My father and the librarian. That is some seriously powerful, *fate* magic."

"Seriously. Those fates," Bygul said.

Muezza let out a snort of agreement.

"They're the worst," Tivali said. "Always taking the credit when it belongs to the goddesses."

"Or more to the point, the matchmaking cats of the goddesses," Soraya said.

"Exactly so," Bygul said.

"IF YOU'RE GOING BACK TO THE EARTH REALM, I'm coming with you," Lucinda announced, making Luc groan.

Seriously, was he ever going to get time alone with his mate? Sure, they'd just spent several days together, but they hadn't had a chance to talk, not even once, not really.

And now, his mate wanted to go back to the earth realm when he hadn't even had a chance to convince her to stay with him in Hell.

"Why are they going back?" Merry asked.

"To attend the book club," Yaro answered.

"What's a book club?"

Oh, great.

Luc rolled his eyes because he knew exactly what was about to happen.

Yep.

Jane immediately launched into a highly descriptive explanation of what a book club was.

Since Merry had never been interested in books, Luc wasn't surprised when her eyes glazed over within seconds of Jane's spiel.

"Okay, so why don't we head on over," Luc said, "and you guys can join us there." It was a brilliant plan, really. He could use the flames to take them wherever he wanted and he was thinking he'd pop them into Jane's apartment above the library. They'd take a bit of time together before going down just in time for the start of this Book Club.

Of course, he could always count on his family to screw things up.

"We'll take the library crossing," Merry said.

"The library?" Jane perked up.

"Dad's library. It has a crossing to yours."

"So that's how everyone kept showing up in the library."

"The witches said there weren't any realm crossings anywhere in Zero, Kansas," Talon protested.

"Well, technically, it's not a crossing," Merry said. "It's a pocket."

"You built a pocket between Hell and Earth?" Tempest asked incredulously.

"Yep. It was so much fun."

"It's pretty high-level magic is what it is."

"Impressive, right? Come on, I'll show you!" Merry jumped up and led the way out of the room, Tempest following, with their mates right behind her.

"This is going to be so much fun!" Lucinda ruffled

Lassiter's hair as she walked by, saying, "Come on, brother. Time for another adventure." She led the way out of the room, Yaro and the other demons following meekly behind.

Lassiter rolled his eyes, helped Jasmine and Starlight to their feet, then the three of them left as well, Jinx and Rebel hitching rides on Jasmine's shoulders.

Luc let out a loud, annoyed groan, then stood. "I guess we're all going. If I leave them to wander through my library on their own, I may have no books left when I go back."

"I thought you said your family wasn't much for reading," Jane said.

"Oh, they're not. They'll just enjoy torturing me by stealing my books."

"Okay, Soraya. I can't believe I'm saying this, but you are a genius," Bygul said, "because I would *never* have matched those two."

"Me neither," Tivali said.

"I'm still uncertain how the two of them match so

well in person, when on paper, it's just absurd," Muezza said.

Soraya twitched her tail at him and said, "It's not absurd. A librarian with the Beast of Hell? It's absolute poetry."

"I never would have believed it if I hadn't seen it with my own eyes," Tivali said. "Oh, my goddess, did you see how Lucifer's library *shifted* when he led her inside?"

"Oh, yeah," Muezza said. "It was incredible."

"Shh," Soraya hissed. "I think it's about to do it again."

"I thought you said you didn't have any novels?" Jane called from several aisles away, where she was exploring his collection.

The minute she'd caught sight of the rows and rows of books, she'd abandoned him to go exploring. Even his admonishment that they might be late for her book club wasn't enough to end her explorations.

Now, she was stamping back, a look of determination on her face.

She grabbed his hand and dragged him around the corner. "Look! You do too have novels. You were just messing with me, weren't you?"

Luc stared, mouth agape, at the opening that had once been the outside wall of his library.

It was now a huge room with one entire wall of windows and two of walls covered in shelves of books.

"Come on." She dragged him down the aisles, pointing out the various genres. "That whole section is mysteries, that row is science fiction and fantasy, this one is horror, this whole wall is romance and this entire section is paranormal romance." She whirled to face Luc. "They're all brand new books, none have been opened. Did you build this room just for me?"

Luc wanted to take credit, but he had to admit, "If I'd thought of it, I would have, but I think it was Hell House itself."

"Hell House?"

"It's what we call the Demon Stronghold. Every Demon is welcome within its walls, but it only responds to the wishes of the Demonic Royalty."

Jane just stared at him. "You'd better not be telling me that you're the King of Hell because I just cannot deal with that."

Luc grinned. "Well, you're in luck because Hell doesn't have a king. It has a Lord, though, and that's me." He sketched a bow. "Lord of the Nine Realms of Hell, at your service. And a lady. That's you. My lady Jane of the Nine Realms of Hell." With that statement, he hauled her into his arms and kissed her.

JANE WOULD HAVE PROTESTED THE TITLE, BUT then Lucifer was kissing her and all thoughts of protesting went out the window as heat barreled through her and she kissed him back for all she was worth.

"Are you guys coming or what?" Merry exclaimed from behind them.

Lucifer let out a growl, causing shivers to run up and down Jane's spine, before pulling away. "To be continued," he muttered against her lips, making her smile.

"Definitely," she whispered back.

"Fine, Merry. Lead the way." They followed Merry back into the main room of the library, where to Jane's amazement, Merry reached down and grabbed a tiny door Jane hadn't even noticed before, and jerked it so that it sprang high and they all walked through it into another room.

The door collapsed behind them and Jane immediately stepped forward to start perusing the titles of books on the shelves in front of her.

She didn't recognize the room or the books, so she knew they hadn't made it back to her library yet.

"Do you like my gift for you, Dad?" Merry asked.

Jane glanced at Lucifer and saw a stunned look on his face. "Gift?"

"The pocket library. You can scoop up either doorway, slide it in your pocket and have access to your library anywhere you go."

"Ooh, like a Kindle, only better because you can feel the books and smell the pages," Jane exclaimed.

"Okay, whatever that is," Merry said. "So, do you like it, Dad?"

Lucifer stepped forward, hooked an arm around Merry's shoulders and pulled her into his arms.

Jane grinned at the stunned look on Merry's face as Lucifer hugged her tight.

"I love it, baby," he said.

Jane couldn't help but be impressed. If Lucifer loved books as much as Jane did—and based on his reaction, she suspected he did—Merry couldn't have given her father a better gift if she'd tried.

"Oh, great." Tempest stepped into the room from another doorway and glared at her father and sister. "I'm guessing you gave him his gift. So rude of you not to include me, Merry. I'll never be able to top this!"

Merry just smirked at her, but Lucifer held out an arm to Tempest, curled her into their hug and said, "What have I been telling you two since you were in diapers?"

"It's not a competition," Tempest and Merry chorused.

"Exactly."

It turned out the pocket library wasn't the only thing that was new in Library Zero.

A mysterious benefactor—Jane suspected Lucifer, though he insisted he'd had nothing to do with it— had funded a full overhaul of the Library's shelving system and inventory and somehow in the three days she'd been gone, everything had changed.

The hardwood floors had been sanded and refinished until they shone.

The old, rickety, metal bookshelves had disappeared in favor of newly constructed, solid, wooden ones that gave the building a true sense of being a library.

The collections had been updated, new books now intermingling with older ones, while the ancient tomes were either set up in display cases or recycled depending on their value to the system.

Everywhere Jane looked, she saw evidence of her dreams come to life.

When she'd asked how it happened, no one seemed to know.

"Perhaps Hell House reached through the pocket library and impacted your realm too," Lucinda speculated. "It's never happened before, but then the Lord of the Nine Realms has never mated someone *not* of the Nine Realms."

"So, what do we have to do to get you ready for your book club, Jane?" Yaro asked.

Jane quickly ran through what needed to be done. "It's Valentine's Day, so everything needs to be red and heart-themed."

Yaro didn't blink an eye, just turned to the other demons and started handing out directions. Within moments, all of Lucifer's demons were hard at work, setting everything up.

"We're going to head out, Jane." Starlight gave her a hug. "Keep in touch, okay?"

"I will. You too."

"Jane, is it okay if Jinx and Rebel come with me?" Jasmine asked.

Jane smiled down at the little girl who reminded her so much of herself at that age.

At least this little girl had a family who would know she wasn't making up stories when she talked about pixies.

"It's completely up to the pixies," Jane said, "but if they want to go home with you, I think that's exactly what they should do."

Jasmine grinned and jumped up and down in excitement. "Did you hear that guys? You get to come with me!"

"Yay! Bye, Janey," the pixies chorused from Jasmine's shoulders as she walked between her parents out of the library.

As if that was the signal to the rest of them, Lucifer's family members began to approach, one-by-one, to wish them congratulations, before heading out.

"Typical," Lucifer muttered when the last of them had left. "There's work to be done and my siblings and daughters all bail. Should have thought to put them to work a long time ago. We'd have finished our mating conversation by now."

Jane grinned at him. "No time like the present, right?"

Lucifer's eyes lit up. "Right." Hooking an arm around Jane's waist, he yanked her into his chest and with a whoosh of flames, flashed them upstairs into her bedroom.

From there, he settled Jane onto her back and came down over her, an intent look on his face.

"So," he murmured against her lips, "how are you feeling about being my mate?"

She smiled, laced her fingers behind his neck and said, "I read paranormal romances by the truckload. In fact, I was planning to spend Valentine's Day reading my latest acquisitions. Instead, I woke in the arms of my fated mate and we've spent the entire day together. How do you think I feel?"

He wrinkled his brow in confusion.

She smiled. "I'm stunned and amazed and delirious with joy."

"Even though your fated mate is the Devil himself?"

"Not even though. *Because.* Lucifer, you're an incredible man, Devil, Beast, Lord, and I'm honored and blessed to be your mate, no matter what your title or form. Let me say it again. I am so happy to have *you*, the Devil, Lord of the Nine Realms and The Beast, as my fated mate."

"Ah, Jane, you fill my heart to overflowing. Happy Valentine's Day, my love." He captured her lips in a searing kiss as the flames of Hell raged around them, burning the world, then reforming it over and over again, as their passion flared bright.

"Who in the world are *you*?" The man who had just stepped into the library stared agape at Yaro, who towered over him.

"I'm Yaro. Who are you?"

"Mr. Higgins. I run the hardware store. I'm here for the book club."

"Well, come on in, Mr. Higgins. Jane should be down soon. Would you like some wine while you wait?"

"I suppose that'd be all right."

IT WAS TRULY THE FUNNIEST THING LUCIFER had ever seen, and that included the day his mate sweet talked his demons into getting library cards and checking out actual books.

By the time he led Jane down the stairs and into the library to attend her book club, things were already well underway.

Someone had arranged the chairs in a circle and demons were interspersed with humans, all of them chatting amiably. Even seated, his demons towered over the humans, not that anyone seemed to mind.

One of the humans stood to get more snacks and Lucifer's eyes widened. "Now that's just wrong." The human's chair was made up of two giant, red hearts, with one forming the back of the chair and the other its seat.

Lucifer shifted slightly to the left and—yep. Every chair had those ridiculous hearts on them. "They should be ashamed of themselves," he muttered to Jane. "No self-respecting demon should ever sit on a heart-shaped chair."

Jane's giggle lifted his spirits, even as his horror

grew. "They're eating heart-shaped snacks, Jane," he growled. "*My* demons, the fiercest demons of the Underworld, are drinking from heart-shaped wine glasses, eating heart-shaped snacks and setting their asses on top of giant red hearts. It's madness, I tell you."

Jane's only response was more giggles.

He wanted to ask her if she'd actually purchased such ridiculous things, but he was afraid her answer might be no, which would mean his *demons* had conjured such absurdities.

Better not to ask, he decided.

He was so disturbed that it took him a moment to realize the humans and demons were engaged in a lively debate about which book deserved to be named the best read of the month.

An elderly gentleman seemed in favor of a futuristic mystery involving a homicide detective while a frail-looking woman, who Lucifer would guess was somewhere in her 90s, insisted that an MC romance was the best of the month.

"What's MC stand for?" Lucifer muttered to Jane.

"Motorcycle Club."

He had no idea what that was—why would a motorcycle need a club—but he was too busy being astonished by his demons to wonder much about it.

As the debate raged on, his demons carefully wrote down the titles and authors of the books the humans were recommending, all while fiercely defending the horror books they'd checked out a few days before, that they'd apparently actually *read*!

"I don't get it," he said to Jane. "I've been trying to get them to read forever, but they never got past a couple pages because they said the books were too boring. Now they've all read hundreds of pages in a few days? What kind of witchcraft is this?"

Jane laughed. "It's called fiction, Lucifer."

Furry and Catsy stalked the perimeter of the library, branding their territory with carefully placed scorch marks.

Paw marks in every corner.

Claw marks down every wall.

It took quite some time, especially when Catsy decided the corners and walls weren't enough and they should also mark each and every aisle.

So they carefully padded along, moving from

bookcase to bookcase, scorching one tiny paw mark at the bottom of every one.

They pondered leaving a mark on every shelf, too, but decided to leave that task for another day.

Once they were satisfied their territory had been sufficiently claimed, they stealthily climbed to the top of the highest bookshelf and stretched out there, side-by-side, front paws hanging over the side of the shelf, and from there, stood guard as their humans joined a lively debate about books and other ridiculous things.

Don't miss Lucinda's story, coming up next,
in *Catanic Rituals.*

A Beautiful Cat-ship

Going Catty

Grave Cattitude

MURRYSVILLE COALITION

The Crazy Cheetah Lady

One Sad Kitty

SHENANIGANS

Shifter Shenanigans

Witchy Shenanigans

Full Moon Shenanigans

Hotel Shenanigans

Dragon Shenanigans

Undercover Shenanigans

Spooky Shenanigans

Holiday Shenanigans

Valentine Shenanigans

Lucky Shenanigans

STORIES OF THE VEIL

Guardians of the Veil

Astra

Glory

Luna

Zara

Guardians of the Realms

WICKED

No Rest for the Wicked

Wicked Is As Wicked Does

About the Author

WWW.PEPPERMCGRAW.COM

PEPPER MCGRAW is a USA Today Bestselling Author of paranormal romance. Her life to date has sadly been paranormal-free, but she expects that will change in time. Until then, she keeps herself busy writing (and reading) paranormal romances.

Pepper loves animals, especially cats, and spends her free time volunteering at local shelters and for Trap-Neuter-Release programs. She's had the supreme honor of winning occasional head butts and meows from the community cats in her neighborhood and has even convinced a few to come inside and adopt her as their own.

amazon.com/author/peppermcgraw

bookbub.com/authors/pepper-mcgraw

facebook.com/ShenanigansSeries

goodreads.com/peppermcgraw

instagram.com/peppermcgraw_author

tiktok.com/@peppermcgraw

x.com/peppermcgraw